BLACKBRIAR

William Sleator

Marshall Cavendish

Marshall Cavendish *Classics*

Marshall Cavendish is bringing classic titles from children's literature back into
print for a new generation. We have selected titles that have withstood the test of
time, and we welcome any suggestions for future titles in this program. To learn
more, visit our Web site: www.marshallcavendish.us/kids.

Marshall Cavendish Corporation
99 White Plains Road
Tarrytown, NY 10591
www.marshallcavendish.us/kids

Library of Congress Cataloging-in-Publication Data

Sleator, William.
    Blackbriar / by William Sleator. — 1st Marshall Cavendish Classics ed.
        p. cm.
    Summary: In the attempt to decipher a number of strange events after he moves
into an old cottage, an orphaned teenaged boy discovers a group of English folk
engaged in Devil worship.
    ISBN 978-0-7614-5585-1
    [1. Supernatural—Fiction. 2. Orphans—Fiction. 3. England—Fiction.] I. Title.
    PZ7.S6313Bl 2009
    [Fic]—dc22
                                        2008044747

Printed in China
1 3 5 6 4 2
ITC Marshall Cavendish

For Siang Chitsa-Ard
1961–2008

LONDON

1

Danny ran in the London twilight. He dodged among the crowds brandishing their large black umbrellas, darted across the path of an angry black taxi, and turned from the main thoroughfare into the darkness of the side street on which he lived. Past one façade he hurried, the same columned porch repeated endlessly down the curving row of connected houses. He was out of breath now, for he tired quickly, but he would not allow himself to stop running. He hated to think what would happen if Philippa reached home before he did.

There were no lights coming from the windows of the second-floor apartment, and he nearly choked with relief. He knew that he could always see a light when Philippa was there. Fumbling with his wet books and his keys, he let himself into the first-floor hall. The stairway ahead of him, covered with a faded red carpet, was so dark that he could barely see to the first landing. "Dammit!" he said petulantly to himself, "why doesn't somebody fix that light?"

He hated the dark. And although it was a relief to know that Philippa would not be home, he was apprehensive as he made his way slowly up the narrow unlit stairs. There was no light switch just inside the apartment door, and when he entered in the dark there were always several moments of near panic while he groped for the cord that hung from the ceiling, blind and vulnerable to whatever he imagined might be waiting in the shadows.

He struggled briefly with the key, then felt it catch and cautiously pushed open the heavy door. The only light in the apartment was pale and gray, coming in dimly through the long windows far at the end of the hallway.

Danny moved toward the center of the room, reaching above his head. Where *was* that cord? His hand grabbed frantically at empty air.

Suddenly he froze. What was that noise? It sounded like a creak, or a footstep. Too terrified to move, he stood with his hand outstretched.

And then there was a thump behind him, and a weight on his shoulder.

Danny shrieked, and in that instant his hand found the cord. The light went on, and a silver Siamese cat leapt delicately from his shoulder to the floor.

"Islington!" Danny cried. "You monster!" and he kicked the cat halfway across the room. "She always takes you to work with her!" he shouted after the animal, who was disdainfully hurrying away. "Why didn't she take you today?"

Danny slammed his books down on a table and sank

weakly into a chair. His knees were shaking so much that he could barely stand. For a moment he just sat and listened to the mad banging of his heart; but very soon he struggled out of the chair and hurried off to his room. Philippa would be home any minute now, and he wanted her to think he had been in the apartment all afternoon.

By the time Philippa did arrive, half an hour later, Danny was in bed, half asleep under piles of blankets. His bed was the only warm place in the apartment, for he was forbidden to light the coal fire in the sitting room until Philippa came home. Perhaps, if the apartment had been warm, he would have spent the time out of bed, reading, or doing his schoolwork. Perhaps not.

When the door slammed down the hall, the window beside his bed rattled, jolting him fully awake.

"There, there, my darling, I know you're starving, I know." Philippa's voice, purring to Islington, floated into Danny's room amid the clatter of parcels dropping to the floor. "Hello!" she called. "Anybody home?"

"I'm here," Danny answered irritably. There was hardly anything he hated more than getting out of a warm bed into a cold room. It was not only the discomfort he minded. He found it very painful to give up the world of half sleep, where he could make almost anything happen merely by thinking about it, for the real world of cold and exertion, where nothing beautiful or exciting ever seemed to happen and everything required effort. But he knew that Philippa was expecting him in the kitchen, and he didn't want her to know that he had been in bed. He unwrapped himself slowly from the blankets and stopped in the bathroom to splash some icy water on his face.

Philippa was at the stove, boiling a fish for Islington. Her earrings shook, her graying hair hung in untidy wisps and strands about her face, and her cheeks sagged. "Oh, hello, darling," she said as he wandered into the room. "I'm sorry I'm so late, but I had to spend hours waiting with that little Mumby boy, whose mother never showed up. Poor little thing, he's too small to get home by himself. At the end I had to send him home in a cab. We had a good time together though. Aside from that, my day's been bloody awful."

"What happened?" Danny slumped into a chair.

"Oh, it's that school!" said Philippa. "How I'll ever make myself set foot in it again I can't imagine!"

Again? Danny thought, preparing himself for a long harangue. "What was it this time?" It was hardly a question.

She looked past him for a moment toward the flat enameled dish under the sink. "Before I start, be a love and empty Islington's toilet. It's so full he can't bear to go in it, and I can tell he's in agony."

The cat lay comfortably under the table, licking his paw. Danny forced himself not to kick him again as he went by. He disliked any kind of physical exertion, particularly carrying things; but he quickly brought the large smelly tray down the two flights of steps and outside into the winter rain, where he dumped its contents into a dustbin. Islington seemed to smirk at him when he got back.

The fish was cooling now, and Philippa had begun to prepare their meal. With her usual quick busyness she was doing something to last night's roast beef. She looked up at him, smiling. "I hope you like what I'm making tonight, dear. It's a new dish I've just thought up. We must try to spark up that nonexistent appetite of yours."

Danny mumbled something incoherent. Food did not interest him.

"If it weren't for you," she went on, "I'd be having a boiled egg and a cold potato, you know." She sighed. "And it does get a bit dreary making all this effort just for you, with never any response." She waited, but he said nothing. Her lips tightened. "And by the way," she said, her voice losing some of its warmth, "did you see anyone after school today?"

Oh, no, Danny thought, and slowly began filling Islington's tray with ashes. "No," he said quietly.

"Oh, come off it now, darling. You know you can't lie to me. I *saw* you walking off today with that Tony Bramble. What?"

He continued to fill the tray as slowly as he could, not looking at her. "Well," he said finally, standing up, "yes, I believe I did."

"There! I *knew* you'd tell me. Now, I've told you before I don't like that boy, and I would rather you didn't see him."

Danny sighed and slouched back into the chair. Who *do* you like? he felt like saying, but instead he said, faintly, "But *I* like him."

"Oh, Danny love, you're so young, you don't know who you like. One thing you've got to learn about life is that most people just aren't worth knowing. Including Tony Bramble. Of course, if it doesn't make any difference to you at all what I think, if it doesn't bother you to make me suffer,"—now her voice was beginning to get that hard edge to it which was always a prelude to a scene,—"if you insist on being so stubborn that you cannot make the smallest concession to the person who has brought you up and taken care of you and fed you and loved you—"

Danny was squirming. "Oh, all right," he interrupted, "I won't see him any more."

Philippa stepped over to him and stooped to kiss his forehead. Her eyes were wet. "My darling boy," she said softly, after a pause, "I know you think I'm unfair. But I am right, you know." She returned to the stove and went on briskly again. "Of course, this isn't to say that one mustn't try one's best to get along with the people one is forced to deal with in the course of a day. That's where I have my problems. I'll never get along with Mr. Dinsdale, never, even if he is the school principal. But what can I do? I can't risk losing that job, can I, dear?" She looked at him sideways. "My job," she repeated when he didn't answer. "You don't think I should quit, do you?"

"What?" Danny said. "Quit your job? Oh, no."

"Yes," she said, "I couldn't quit. Of course, if one had money," she added dreamily. "If one had money, and servants too, the way one grew up . . ." She was always "one" in the past; but she never said any more than a few words about it, always finishing, as now, with "But that's the past. No use thinking about that," and going on. "No, I couldn't quit my job. Not that I wouldn't be overjoyed never to set foot in that bloody school again. I'd adore dashing off into some new, wild life, far away from this awful dirty noisy city. And Islington, poor darling, cooped up inside all day, never out chasing mice and things, he could do with a change. I've been in such an awful rut, never . . ."

Danny returned to his thoughts. He never knew what to say when she went on like this, because he was positive she would never have the nerve to quit her job. But sometimes he wondered what would happen to him if she did leave London. At the least, it would mean that he would no longer have to live with her, something he often longed for. He knew that it was useless for him to suggest that perhaps he should move out, for he would be unable, as always, to stand up to the threats and cajolings and protestations she would make. But if she should leave London . . . She'll never leave, he told himself.

He remembered how it had been when he first came to live with her. He had never known his father, who had died shortly after he was born. His early childhood, with only his mother, had been warm and very sheltered. But when he was seven his mother had died suddenly, leaving him a small annuity, no relatives, and a busy, indifferent lawyer as his guardian. Philippa Sibley, the secretary at his school, had always befriended a certain special few of the younger children; and though Danny was not a particularly good student, his wild imagination had intrigued her. On that awful day, when word had come to the office that he no longer had a mother or a home to go to, it had been the most natural thing in the world for Philippa to take him back to her large kitchen, give him hot chocolate, and talk to him in a rich, soothing voice. Since there was nowhere else for him to go, there he had stayed. And when Mr. Bexford, the lawyer, finally found time to deal with Danny, it had been the simplest (and quickest) solution to allow him to remain with Philippa.

She was certainly qualified to bring up a child. Not only had she worked at the school for many years, but she had had her own family. She was a widow now, and her only child, a daughter, had gone to South America at eighteen and never returned. Philippa assured Mr. Bexford that Danny would certainly not be a bother, that his annuity would be ample for room and board, and it had all been settled. The check that arrived punctually once a year was all they had heard from him since.

As Danny had grown older he had become rather dissatisfied with the arrangement. And now, at fifteen, he saw that other children were beginning to grow away from their parents. Philippa had met the few token attempts he had made at semi-independence with hysterical scenes, threats, and accusations. He had given in quickly, vaguely resentful, but unwilling to continue to provoke her anger. It was so much easier and less painful simply to adjust. And there *is* a lot that's good about her, he would tell himself. Any other place I lived would probably be worse.

He had grown quite used to her, after all.

". . . trudging back to this dreary flat on this dreary street. Never admitting to myself how much I really hate this kind of life. But now that I've found out about this place, it might be possible to break away." She sat down across from him. "Danny? Didn't you hear me? I said, now that I've found out about this place, it might be possible for me to break away."

"What? What place? What do you mean?"

"I never mentioned it before because I didn't know if I'd ever have the nerve to do anything about it. But I suppose I might as well tell you anyway." She paused, as if she were about to reveal something precious and very secret. She looked away from him for a moment, then pursed her lips.

"There's a little house, a cottage, far away from London, near the sea. It's very old, no one knows how old, and very secluded, miles away from the nearest tiny village. Nobody knows why it is there, so far away from everything else, with only a rough road leading to it. And no one has lived there for as long as anyone can remember. It's on a wooded, rocky hillside, and the farmer who owns the land is looking for someone to buy the place so he can get some profit out of it. But no one will live there, I suppose because it is so secluded."

"But how did you find out about it?"

"The farmer advertises it in *Country Life*. The ad has been running there for years and years, and I never paid much attention to it. But then, a few weeks ago, Mr. Braintree from the school, who also gets *Country Life*, told me he'd seen the place, quite by accident, when he was on holiday. He was out walking and saw this strange little house, and realized it must be the same place. You should have heard him go *on* about it—"

"I hear him go on plenty in biology every day."

"But oh, it sounds so beautiful! It's on a high ridge, and you can see the ocean and miles all around. It has flint walls, yellow lichen on the roof, and a huge chimney. He looked in through the windows, and he could scarcely see for the dust, and of course the place was a *mess*, but he could make out a huge stone fireplace, and thick beams, and a narrow, winding stairway. He would have taken it himself, he said, but it wasn't big enough for his family. "Oh," she sighed, "if only, if *only* I had the nerve to do something about it!"

"But why do you want to live so far away from everything?"

"Why, I love the country! It's so much nicer than this awful dirty noisy city. You've always lived in the city, you have no idea what the country is like."

"And you'd really like to live in such a secluded place all by yourself?" he said skeptically.

"I'd have Islington." She lowered her eyes. "And of course, *you* could come too, darling, if you liked."

"Me?" Then he noticed the expression on her face, and suddenly began to be afraid. Could she really mean it? Then I'd *really* never be able to live anywhere else, he groaned inwardly. And how cold and uncomfortable it would be! "But this is ridiculous," he said. "You couldn't afford to buy a house."

"Perhaps I could. I have been putting a little away over the years. And your annuity would help."

"But . . . but I couldn't go with you. I have to go to school. I don't exactly love it, but it would be rather hard to get out of, wouldn't it?"

"We could work it, dear. You've passed your 'O' levels, after all. A lot of boys your age take a year's holiday. You could certainly use it. And I could certainly educate you as well as any of those so-called teachers."

"But what about Mr. Bexford?" He was trying to keep

his voice down. "What would he say? He wouldn't let me leave school. And anyway, I *like* London," he said helplessly. "I don't *want* to go hiding away in the country!"

"Islington's hungry," Philippa said. The cat was pawing at her lap, whining for his fish. The room had become very dark, and they could hear the clatter of dishes from the apartment across the way. "I suppose it's time for us to eat, too," she added, standing up.

2

The train pulled slowly away from Victoria Station. From inside the compartment Danny watched porters, baggage carts, and iron pillars slide by. In a moment they were outside, the vast, arching black cage diminishing behind them. Even more quickly they passed the Battersea power station, darkening the sky with its dense, billowing clouds of filth. Rows and rows of tenements, crouching up against the track, whizzed by, twisted and crowded together into one continuous, miserable pattern. And though the train had gained considerable speed, for a long time the tenements did not let go, but kept clutching at the train for mile after mile, trying to pull it back into the city.

"I can't understand why it takes so long to get away," Danny said, "why places like this go on and on, almost as if people *liked* them."

"*We* got away," Philippa said from across the aisle. "We

got away, incredibly enough, and I, for one, am going to stay away. I already feel ten years younger." She was surrounded by bulging canvas bags containing blankets, sheets, curtains, and tablecloths from the London flat. Cardboard boxes full of crockery, silverware, and glasses rattled precariously on the rack above her head. Battered suitcases, splitting at the seams, took up most of the other space in the compartment. Islington prowled on the floor, sniffing at the feet of the other occupants of the compartment, three uneasy people whose baggage lay outside in the corridor. They were an elderly couple and a prim young lady, who had already established a kind of rapport, and regarded Philippa and Danny with wary curiosity.

Philippa reached over and patted Danny's wrist. "I'm sure you're going to love it in the country," she said. "Don't sulk like that."

"I'm not sulking," he said, drawing away his hand. "I'm just wondering what's going to happen when Mr. Bexford finds out about this."

"But what can he do, darling? He'll never find us."

"I'm sure he'll get in touch with the school."

"They won't even know you're gone until winter holidays are over, and by that time they'll never be able to trace us. And anyway, *I'm* going to educate you, so they really have no reason to object. Cheer up! It's ridiculous for someone of your age to be so worried. I'll be held responsible, after all. Just look at the whole thing as an adventure."

The tenements had finally fallen away, and the winter landscape outside was beginning to shake off the city grime.

A black frozen river twisted between brown hills, occasionally spanned by a crumbling stone bridge. Groups of barren trees stood naked under the heavy sky, as if huddling together for warmth; but the clusters of fir trees that seemed to be everywhere gave the scene an uncanny feeling of green.

Danny and Philippa gazed out of the windows, absorbed by the open landscape, by a sky not hidden behind buildings and smoke. But Islington did not care about the sky, and poked restlessly about the floor of the compartment. Suddenly he leapt up onto the young lady's lap and crouched there, staring intently into her face. She coughed, and shifted about, and tried to look away from his burning eyes. But, fascinated by this new human being, he did not move.

She coughed again. "Excuse me," she said, "but your cat . . ."

Philippa turned from the window. "Islington!" she barked. "Islington, get down! Bad boy!" The cat spun around, hesitated, and jumped down. Philippa picked him up and shook him gently. "Bad boy!" she said. "Bad, bad boy. I'm *so* sorry," she said to the young lady, without a trace of apology in her voice.

"It's quite all right," the lady said, brushing silvery hairs from her blue coat. The elderly couple looked at each other, then into their laps.

The train rumbled and shook. A tiny stone village rushed by. No one said a word.

"He's hungry," Philippa said suddenly. "That's what's wrong with him. Poor thing, cooped up in this compartment.

Danny, get down that box up there on the left. It has the food in it."

Swaying, Danny stood up on the seat. He stretched to reach the heavy box, and barely managed to set it down next to her without dropping it. Philippa dug into the box and finally unearthed a round plastic dish with foil over the top. She uncovered the dish and set it on the floor near her feet. A rank, fishy smell filled the compartment. The young lady looked away, dusting her nose with a white handkerchief. But the elderly couple were watching Islington. He sniffed at the fish, poked it with his paw, and tasted a bit. But soon he turned away restlessly.

"*I* know," Philippa said. "He has to go to the toilet." Danny quickly turned and stared out the window. He tried to keep sulking, but it was almost impossible not to laugh. Philippa, in a very business-like manner, covered the fish and put it away, then spread newspaper on the floor between her and Danny. The young lady and the old couple could not keep their eyes away, and watched, transfixed with horror, as Islington circled around on the paper, then settled down comfortably.

But in a moment he was up and walking around again, and the paper was clean. There was an audible sigh of relief from the other side of the compartment. Philippa folded the paper, and then held Islington on her lap, stroking him.

The train began to slow down, and came to a stop beside a small wooden platform with a slanting tile roof above it. One or two ruddy-cheeked people with steaming breath stood about on the platform, searching the train windows for expected faces. In a moment they were joined by their friends, there was a distant, unintelligible shout, and the train creaked to a start, slowly gathering momentum. More fields flashed by, and then suddenly a gray, walled castle clinging to the pinnacle of a steep hill. Below it a wide river ran past a timbered inn and a small cluster of wooden houses.

Danny found that he was fascinated by the scenery. Why did it seem so beautiful, so mysterious? It was only farmland, but to him it was a wilderness. Were those the eyes of a wolf pack glittering behind that clump of trees? Perhaps that bristly shape was a wild boar, sharpening his tusk against a pine. A hut with a sagging roof became the abode of a wizened hag, mumbling incantations over a cauldron. And who knew what strange creatures roamed in the darkness beneath the trees?

He felt a soft, warm weight in his lap and involuntarily shrank back. Philippa was digging into the box by her side and had put Islington out of her way for a moment. Danny sat uncomfortably, trying to touch the cat as little as possible. He knew that Islington shared his distaste; but somehow he felt that the cat, as he did, passively submitted to this unwelcome contact simply because it was expedient. It would have made everything more difficult for either of them to object.

Philippa took out two round, hollow pieces of Syrian bread, a bag filled with pieces of chicken, and another with cucumber and tomato slices. She closed the box and laid the food on top, then brought Islington back into her lap. Leaning over, she whispered to Danny, "I wonder if the other people will mind."

"Do you really care?" he whispered back. "After the spectacle you made with Islington . . ."

"That was different. I just feel awkward eating in front of people and not offering them some."

"Offer them some, then."

"After the way she treated Islington?"

"It was *your* idea to eat. If you didn't want to, why did you take out the food?"

She handed Danny one of the pieces of bread and opened the two bags. Rocking with the motion of the train, they began to stuff the bread with the chicken and vegetables. It wasn't easy, but eating them was even more difficult. Tiny pieces of chicken, tomato seeds, and juice dropped to the floor. Danny could not keep his eyes from slipping frequently to the other side of the compartment, but the others seemed to be ignoring them. Islington, at least, was having a good time knocking the scraps about.

They passed many stations, the train stopped many times, and the others had all left before they heard the conductor call out "Dunchester!" and the train again began to slow down. There was a brief but chaotic time of scratches and grunts, draggings, liftings, pantings, and hysterical commands. They suddenly found themselves amid piles of crushed baggage on a tiny, unfamiliar platform. The train creaked around a hill and was gone.

3

"The man from the local garage was *supposed* to meet us with a car," Philippa said.

They had dragged the luggage through the small, dusty waiting room and out to the front of the station. It was on a narrow cobblestone street across from a few little shops. There was a butcher shop with big slabs of red meat in the window, a whole pig, and a row of feathered birds hanging upside down above them. Next to it was a bakery with a window full of cakes and rolls. As they watched, a young girl set out a tray of steaming, freshly baked bread.

Danny sat down on a suitcase. "As long as we're waiting," said Philippa, "I might as well dash across the street and pick up some food." She dropped Islington into his lap, slung her handbag over her shoulder, and went into the butcher's. As he struggled with the squirming cat, Danny watched her through the shop window chatting with a white-haired man in a big white apron, who talked and laughed as he sawed off pieces of meat, plucked down strings of sausages, and wrapped them in brown paper. But suddenly the man stopped smiling. He seemed to have a serious expression on his face, and Philippa seemed to be at a loss for words. When she came out of the shop she gave Danny a strange look from across the street and darted into the bakery. There she talked to the ladies behind the counter, and they too suddenly became oddly serious. When she came back to the station, loaded down with parcels, she seemed slightly nervous.

"What did they say to you?" Danny asked.

She remained standing, clutching at the packages of food. "It's the strangest thing," she said. "They were all the pleasantest people, so much friendlier than people in London shops. And the food seems so good, and the prices are so low! But when I told them we were going to be living in the little cottage up on the ridge—they call it Blackbriar around here—they suddenly got all worried and strange."

"But why? What did they say?"

"They hardly said anything. They wouldn't. The butcher just said, 'Oh, so you're living *there*, are you,' and refused to say another word. Naturally the ladies in the bakery were more talkative, but all they said was that no one had lived there for years and years, and everyone talked in this secretive manner. I mean, I would *expect* people to have some superstitions about an empty, secluded place like that. But why wouldn't they say anything about it?"

"Now it's beginning to sound interesting," Danny said.

"I hardly dared to hope that the place would be mysterious. I wonder if it's supposed to be haunted or something?"

"You seem to be taking it very lightly."

"But this might actually make it bearable here."

"You wouldn't be so happy about it if you'd seen their faces."

"And also," he went on, "we're bound to find out what it is about the place, from living there and everything."

"Yes," Philippa said, "I'm sure we are."

It was late afternoon, and very cold. In the fading light, the little street seemed almost deserted. Above the row of shops they could see high hills disappearing into the distance, and black groves of trees silhouetted against the darkly glowing sky. Somewhere, on one of those hills, in one of those groves, was their new home.

Two headlight beams swept across the darkened store fronts, and in a moment a clattering truck pulled up beside the station. A small but sturdily built man jumped out, leaving the lights on and the motor running, and stepped quickly up to them. "Hello," he said, holding out his hand. "I'm Albert Creech, from Creech's garage. Sorry I'm late, but it's hard to know when this train's going to arrive. It's never been on schedule yet."

"Oh, that's all right, Mr. Creech," said Philippa, beaming as she shook his hand. "This is—a pupil of mine, Danny Chilton."

"Pleased to meet you, Danny," said Mr. Creech, and shook his hand. "Shall we load all this stuff into the van, then?"

Mr. Creech supervised, and in a few minutes everything was packed tightly into the back of the little truck. Philippa sat in the front with Islington on her lap, and Danny reclined against soft canvas bags in back.

"It's a pity you got here in the dark," said Mr. Creech, as they rolled off down the street. "You won't be able to see what Dunchester looks like." In the glow of the headlights they could catch only brief glimpses of wooden shop fronts, cobblestone pavements, and the stone buttresses of what must have been a large cathedral. In a moment the town was gone completely. Thick black shapes of trees rose up on either side of them, and the only thing they could see distinctly was the few feet of dirt road ahead.

"Is the Land Rover you found ready for us, Mr. Creech?" asked Philippa. "I'm rather eager to get to the cottage as soon as possible."

"The car's ready, but you certainly won't get up there tonight."

"We won't?" Philippa said. "Why not?"

"You'd never get up to that place at night if you've never driven there before. Why, the road only goes part of the way up the hill. After that you have to drive through a large field, and a bit of forest. With no roads. If you tried it tonight, you'd never make it." He turned for a second to Philippa, then back to the road. "I hope you know what you're getting into, ma'am," he said quietly.

"I thought I did. But now things are beginning to look a little different. I knew it was isolated, but not inaccessible. And . . . Mr. Creech, is there something *wrong* with the place?"

"Why do you ask?"

"Well, the people in the shops seemed . . . surprised that I was going to live there. I might almost say afraid. Is there some superstition surrounding it?"

"Oh, don't take any notice of what *they* say. Those towns-folk never set foot outside the city walls. They couldn't tell an owl from a pheasant. They're just suspicious of the place because it's so far away from everything else. They're afraid of the outdoors, they're afraid to be far away from other people."

"Is that all, Mr. Creech?"

"Well," he said, and then paused, concentrating on the road. "I suppose . . . there's the tumuli, you know. That's the only thing I can think of."

"The tumuli? What's that?"

"They're these . . . mounds. But they're all the way at the other end of the ridge."

"But what *are* they? Why are people afraid of them?"

"I wouldn't say people are afraid of them, exactly. They just don't go near them very often. Supposedly they are the burial mounds of three Druid kings. They're at the narrow end of the ridge and you can see the whole country from there. It's a beautiful place. But, there is a strange feeling about it. As though—as though nature, the outdoors, something, was close around, was stronger there than anywhere else. I'm not good with words. But, to me, it's a feeling I like. And I'd think you two would like it as well, if you want to live so deep in the country. But you can understand why town people would stay away."

"That doesn't sound so bad, does it, Danny?" Philippa said, turning around to him.

"It sounds all right," he said, but he could tell by the expression on her face, and the tone of her voice, that she thought Mr. Creech was leaving something out.

"By the way," she said, turning back, "where *are* we going to stay tonight, since we can't get up to the cottage?"

"Oh, I've arranged that for you. My old folks have a big house across the road from my garage. There's plenty of room there. They've already made up the rooms for you. All your gear will be safe in my van overnight. In the morning we can load it into your Land Rover, and you'll get a good early start. In the daylight."

Danny lay in the back and watched the black shapes move by. His eyes had become adjusted to the darkness, and he could make out where the hills ended and the sky began. He was drowsy, the canvas bags were soft, and he had wrapped a thick blanket around himself. He felt warm and comfortable, so that it was very easy to imagine the distant hills not as dreary, uncomfortable places, but as a mysterious and intriguing new world. Perhaps this won't be so bad, he told himself. At least I don't have to go to school; she may even let me sleep late.

He, too, felt that there was something strange about the place that Mr. Creech did not want to tell them, but he was glad of it. Adventure can seem very attractive to someone who has no idea at all what it really means; and Danny, who had always been taken care of and had never made a decision in his life, knew less about it than most. As he began to drift toward unconsciousness, visions of his life in the country floated haphazardly through his mind. Barefoot, he would creep silently through the forest without disturbing a twig. The deer would become his friends. He would learn the language of the wolves, and teach them to do his bidding. Soon he would never live in the house at all, but would make his home among the trees and in rocky grottos. For miles around, people would whisper about the strange "nature boy," a strong yet faun-like creature, not really human, more like some archaic god . . .

Suddenly they turned and the lights flashed over a pair of old gas pumps. The truck drove into a high-ceilinged garage, littered with tools and reeking of gas, and came to a stop.

"Here we are," said Mr. Creech, and hopped out.

"Danny, bring that little brown bag," said Philippa. "That's all I need for tonight."

Danny carried two bags and Philippa held Islington, who was irritably beginning to wake up, stretching his claws and shaking himself. With the motor off, the silence swelled suddenly around them. Mr. Creech pulled down the garage door and locked it. "I suppose the food will stay fresh in this cold," Philippa said.

"There's plenty to eat inside," said Mr. Creech. "It's just time for supper."

Mr. Creech's beaming pregnant wife and his tiny little girl soon joined them, and they went across the road to the Creeches' old, shingled Victorian house. Inside it was dim and warm. Real wood fires burned in each small room. The meal was tasteless and very heavy. There was shepherd's pie, boiled cabbage, and bread pudding for dessert. Mr. Creech's daughter took a rapid liking to Islington, who reluctantly allowed her to play with him under the table until after dessert, when the little girl emerged with a long scratch on her arm and was given another helping of pudding to ease the pain.

No one said a word about the cottage, almost as if, Danny thought, they didn't want to spoil the evening by mentioning it.

4

In the morning the sun was bright, but there was a high, cold wind. Philippa was eager to see her Land Rover, a kind of jeep, which Mr. Creech had found for her. It was a sturdy little car, the roof and sides made of one sheet of canvas strung over metal poles. It had four-wheel drive, and was the only kind of vehicle, Mr. Creech said, that could get up to Blackbriar. Philippa was enchanted with it. Though it was old and a bit rusty, and the canvas tended to sag, there was a feeling of solidness and security to it. The license plate said LIL, and so Philippa decided that Lil would be her name.

They quickly loaded everything into the back and lashed the canvas down tightly. Philippa sat in the driver's seat, and Danny sat next to her, clutching Islington, who writhed uncomfortably.

"Sorry I can't come with you," said Mr. Creech through the window, "but you can see how busy I am here at the garage. I don't think you'll have much trouble finding it. Just stay on this road, take the right fork, go about ten miles till you come to the Black Swan Inn. Right across the road you'll see a little dirt lane going up the hill. When it ends, go through the gate you'll see, across the field, through the next gate, and then into the forest. There's a track through the trees you can follow. In a few miles you'll be there."

At first they stalled frequently, until Philippa got used to the gears. The car wheezed, and the wind tore violently at the canvas, which billowed around them, penetrating into all the chinks so that it was no warmer than being outside. For the first few miles the road they were on seemed to be below the fields around it. On either side there was a high mound, covered with bushes, which they could not see over. Suddenly Philippa pulled over to the side of the road, up to a small gate.

"This isn't the Black Swan," Danny said.

"No, but I think it's the farmhouse where Mrs. Creech told me she gets those divine eggs we had for breakfast." They left Islington in the car and went through the gate, up a few stone steps, and found themselves in a small garden, full of green plants covered by cheesecloth. The plump old woman who answered the door babbled happily and sold them two dozen eggs and some milk. Danny walked around to the back and saw a beautiful little greenhouse. Behind the house was a large barn, from which came the brittle, demented cackling of hundreds of chickens cooped up together.

Soon Philippa shouted for him and they returned to the car. Around a bend in the road a small forest sprang up.

The trees stood above them, their exposed roots twisting and clutching down the mound of earth, almost to the road. Just as suddenly, the forest disappeared, the mound sank away, and they were driving down the center of a flat, almost tree-less valley, exposed to the wind and the hills towering around them. One hill loomed closer than the rest, its top covered with strange twisted bushes that seemed almost black. "Blackbriar," Philippa said softly.

The Black Swan was a large white house at one end of a small green. Across from it a dirt road wound steeply up the hillside. Philippa turned sharply, and Lil began to pull herself up the slope. Danny looked back and saw the road, the inn, and the cows grazing on the green grow smaller and smaller. Just before the view was hidden by trees he caught a glimpse of a gaunt, gray mansion halfway up the hill.

The road became steeper and less distinct. When it reached the top it turned into a small grove of trees, and ended at a rusty gate. Beyond the gate was a rolling field, scattered with tiny round bumps. Danny hopped out and held the gate open, closing it after the car had gone through. When he climbed back in, his city shoes were covered with dripping mud.

The canvas flapped even more as they started across the field. The car swerved and tilted each time they went over a bump. Islington groaned uncomfortably and dug into Danny's legs with his claws. In the distance was another gate, which Philippa headed for as directly as she could. All around them, beyond the field, they could see only other hilltops. All at once Danny began to realize how isolated they were.

Beyond the second gate was the forest. There was something of a track here, but it was more like a row of deep ruts winding among the trees. The car constantly seemed about to tip over, as Philippa twisted and turned the wheel, slipping with a bounce from one rut into another, trying to avoid thick roots and dead branches that hung across the path. Islington howled and clung to Danny with claws like needles. Crockery and milk bottles rattled, egg cartons and heavy canvas bags slid around in the back. Philippa sat very straight, her hands clutching the wheel, a cigarette clenched in her lips. Danny's door kept swinging open, and he tried to hang on to the back of the seat, to the roof, but there was nothing he could really grab. The car slipped under a low branch which scraped heavily against the canvas. Looking over at Philippa, who was concentrating so intensely, Danny tried to keep from falling out of the car, to keep a hold on Islington without getting his eyes scratched out. He heard a milk bottle crash to the floor just as a canvas bag landed on a carton of eggs. He began to laugh. At first it was only a chuckle, but before he knew it he was out of control, rolling around in the seat, clutching his sides. Philippa was shocked for a second, and then began to laugh herself, which did not improve her driving.

They lumbered through the dense forest in the little battered car, narrowly missing every tree in their way. The grunting of the motor and their hysterical laughter echoed through the deep silence. They did not stop laughing until, around a curve, they found themselves in a wide clearing. Their new home stood before them.

BLACKBRIAR

5

Stark and gray, the old house rose from the ground as if it had grown there.

The car came to a sudden stop and the motor died. Philippa and Danny stepped slowly out. The only sounds were a few lonely bird calls, and the wind.

It was not a large house. The nubbly flint walls were two stories high, broken by only a few narrow windows. The pointed roof was of faded red tiles, covered by a yellowish lichen, and extended for a foot beyond the walls. There were tiles missing in places, and some of the bricks in the two chimneys were gone. It was desolate, it was lonely, it was almost forbidding. Yet it did not seem derelict. There was a feeling of life about the place, as if it had *not* been left for centuries to crumble and decay. Something, Danny felt, was waiting there; and suddenly he had the uncanny sensation that it was waiting for him.

He tried to shake these thoughts away as they walked around the house. It was rectangular in shape. The long side facing over the hill, down through slender scattered trees to hills below, had a few windows. The other long side, with the doorway, faced into a dense pine woods and had no windows at all. Over the doorway was a lopsided arbor made of twisted tree branches, covered with twining brown vines. Philippa took a large key out of her handbag and fitted it into the rusty lock. Neither of them said a word.

The key fit beautifully and the door swung open, squeaking. Cautiously they stepped inside, into a short, narrow passageway only about six feet long. They followed it to the right, into a large room. It was so dark inside that at first they could hardly see a thing. But as their eyes adjusted to the darkness, the room began to take shape around them. They could make out a great stone fireplace against the left wall, with a mantel made of a rough-hewn log. There was a spinning wheel in one corner, and a bookcase built into a wall. In front of the fireplace were two heavy, sagging chairs and a round wooden table. On the other side of the fireplace, behind a door, was a very steep, narrow, winding stairway. And next to this was another door, thick and heavy and ancient. Black iron hinges in strange curving shapes held it to the wall. Danny was fascinated. There seemed to be words carved into the door, but it was too dark to see what they were. Cobwebs, naturally, were everywhere.

Philippa prodded one of the chairs. "Damp," she said. "What this place needs is a good airing." She stepped over to a window, rubbed some dust off the mottled pane with one finger, and pushed it open. Light poured into the room, showing them how dusty the windows were. When they were all opened Danny went back to the ancient door. The carvings were now perfectly clear. "Hey, look at this!" he called. "Come over here!"

Philippa peered over Danny's shoulder. Roughly but deeply carved into the door in an archaic, almost gothic, hand was a list of names. After each name was a date. "Look," he said, reading the names with difficulty, "'Euen Bradley—2 December 1665. Lemuel Greaves—5 December 1665. Patience Falk—20 December 1665. Adam Burnside— 2 January 1666. Anne Ordway—5 January 1666 . . .' It's funny, the dates are all so close together, and they go chronologically. What could it mean? And at the bottom, there's one name without a date at all. Mary Peachy. I wonder what it means?"

Philippa turned away. "Let's go look at the rest of the house," she said. "We've got a lot to do today."

Danny pulled at the iron handle on the door. It scraped slowly open. A gust of cold, moist air blew across his face. Crumbling stone steps led down into impenetrable darkness.

"Come and look at the kitchen," Philippa called. Her voice sounded hollow and distant. Danny pushed the door closed and hurried past the fireplace, through the little passageway and into the kitchen, which was to the left of the front door.

It was a narrow room, but compact and well arranged. The wooden sink was just below the window. Against one wall was a low shelf, which could be used as a working surface, with other shelves below it. Filling the right side of the room was a big black coal stove. Philippa was crouching before it, her head in the oven. When she emerged there was a black smudge on her forehead. "It looks like it's in working order," she said. "I wonder if there's any coal around?" She stood up. "How do you like the sink? I can look out on the hillside while I'm washing the dishes. Or you can."

Past the kitchen was a dining room with a dark red tile floor and a small fireplace. The only furniture was a large oval wooden table with four chairs around it. The chairs were ornately carved with figures of strange beasts, crouching and eating each other.

Another winding stairway led up from this room. They followed it to a small whitewashed bedroom, which led to a larger bedroom, which in turn led to the largest bedroom of all, at the top of the stairway from the living room. The fireplace here was quite large, and there were windows on two walls. Philippa sank down on the lofty iron bed. "This mattress is damp," she said. "It's a good thing there's sun today. We can drag all these things out and let them get dry."

She looked at Danny, who was leaning against the fireplace. "Well, what do you think?"

"I like the door with all those names carved on it," he said. "I wonder if it's really as old as the dates say?"

"But what about the house? Don't you have any feelings about it at all?"

Danny did feel a certain muted excitement, tinged with a pleasurable fear, about living in a place that was so strange and old. But, trying to sound bored, he said, "I suppose it's all right. I just wonder what we're going to do here all the time."

"Oh," she said, tossing her head impatiently, "why do you have to be so damned . . . bloody-minded! Can't you see what this place is? Why, it's a perfectly unspoiled, natural, unique . . . country cottage! Places like this just don't exist any more. It's exactly what I've always dreamed of." Her voice switched from anger to eagerness. "And I already have so many ideas about what we can do with it. This house is crying out for somebody to pull it back into shape. Why—"

Downstairs there was a sudden, rapid scuffling. Philippa almost jumped from the bed. "What was that?"

"Islington?" Danny suggested.

"I made sure he was locked in the car." She looked about nervously. Outside the window there were more trees than Danny had ever seen in his life. It was so cold in the room that he could see his breath.

"Why were all those people so secretive . . . ?" Philippa asked softly. They watched each other for a moment, warily. Then, quickly, Philippa stood up, briskly brushing her tweed skirt. "It must have been a mouse," she said. "We've got to let that poor cat out of the car. And we're wasting precious time just sitting here. If we don't get organized before dark, we'll be in a real muddle."

They dragged down the mattresses from the biggest bedroom and the smallest one and set them out in the sun, along with the living room chairs. With Islington jumping at their heels they carried things in from the car. At first the cat would not enter the house, but waited at the doorway, swinging his tail about nervously and gazing inside. Finally, his nose twitching, he stuck in his head, testing the floor with one paw. When he entered, his back arched for a moment and the fur on his tail stiffened. His head swung back and forth rapidly. "Now why is he acting so strangely?" Philippa asked, pausing with a box of crockery in her arms.

"Aren't cats always cautious like that?" Danny grunted as he heaved a canvas bag full of blankets over to the stairs.

Philippa watched him as he set it down. "Why don't you take the flashlight and go see what's behind that old door," she said, "since it's the only thing you like about the house."

"By myself?" he said quickly, without thinking.

"Islington will go with you. *I've* got to put all these dishes away."

But when, with flashlight in hand, Danny pulled open the heavy door, the cold musty air touched Islington too. He spun away as if he had been hit, his back went up again, he growled and spat and dashed out of the house. Danny switched on the flashlight, and the first thing it brought to light was a pump, standing on the small landing where the stone steps turned. "Hey! A pump!" he shouted.

"Super!" Philippa called from the kitchen. "That must mean there's an underground well. The pump probably brings water up from it to the sink. What luxury!"

He continued slowly down the steps. The air felt heavy and damp, and he could hear water dripping. He began to be afraid. Fear more intense than he had ever known seemed to seep into him with the moist air and the darkness. When he reached the last step he could barely make himself step down onto the stone floor. He flashed the light quickly over the walls, constantly turning to look behind. There were a few rusty bedsprings and crumbling pieces of furniture, some strange, blunt tools hanging on hooks, and in one corner a dusty black pile of coal.

Upstairs, the cellar door slammed shut with a crash. Suddenly his heart was pounding furiously. As quickly as he could he stumbled up the stairs backwards, probing the darkness with the light. But when he reached the top the door would not open. He began to bang on it with his fist, turning around constantly to shine the light back down the stairs. "Hey!" he cried. "Get me out of here! Let me out!"

He heard Philippa's quick steps, then the sound of the latch. At last the door swung open. Her face was full of alarm. "What happened?"

"Nothing," he said, trying to regain his composure. He glared at Islington, who was crouching between Philippa's feet. "The door slammed by itself. I guess it must lock from the outside."

"But what's down there?"

"Oh, just a cellar. There's a big pile of coal in it."

"How marvelous! Would you be a darling and bring some to me? I'd really like to get the stove started, it might be a big job. Oh, and after that, why don't you try pumping for a bit. We've got to find out if that pump brings water up to the sink faucet; nothing comes out when I turn it on now. And I'm dying for a cup of tea."

Danny's ingrained response to Philippa's requests was stronger than his fear. He realized that she was going to ask him to go down there frequently, and decided that he might as well get used to it from the beginning. This time he dashed down the steps, scooped up the coal, and dashed back up in less than a minute. But fear hung in the basement like cobwebs, and even in that brief time it penetrated to his bones.

On the landing he felt a bit more comfortable. Some light reached it from the living room, and he left the flashlight on while he pumped with his back to the wall. He was limp and panting after only thirty strokes. Just when his arms seemed about to fall off, he heard Philippa shriek, "Water! Water!" from the kitchen, and stopped pumping immediately. That will *have* to be enough to last until tomorrow, he told himself.

While Philippa banged and poked at the coal stove, Danny dragged in the mattresses and chairs and made up the beds. When he came back down, the stove was humming and crackling and the kitchen was filling with warmth. The water took a while to boil, but soon they were standing with steaming mugs in their hands, taking brief sips of scalding tea.

"Well, now that we're a little bit organized I feel much better," Philippa said. "But I really can't rest until I get rid of some of this dust and cobwebs."

Danny was looking out the window. "Can't we take a break and go outside? I'd like to see what it's like around here before it gets dark."

"You go, darling. Take a little walk. I really couldn't enjoy it with the place in this condition, and you wouldn't be much help dusting anyway. But don't stay away too long. You'd never find your way back in the dark."

In the clearing there were a few thick trees. At the opposite end from the track on which they had come was another rusting gate. Danny paused there and turned back to look at the house. Under the vastness of the sky, which had become heavy and overcast, the house seemed small and defenseless. Yet there it belonged. It fit into the landscape like another tree, or part of the hillside. It was hard to believe it had been built at all, that it hadn't always been there.

From the gate a path led through a small thicket of pine trees. As he entered he heard a rustling in the underbrush, and what sounded like a strange, choked gasp. He spun around, but could see nothing unusual. It must be some kind of bird, he told himself. But he began walking faster.

The path soon led out of the trees and ended at a wide, grassy track. On the right was a thick forest, and on the left scrub bushes and small twisted trees tumbled down the hillside. Danny realized that this track led right along the top of the long, narrow hill. As he walked he could see occasional pathways leading into the forest. On the other side he knew he should be able to see a view, but he couldn't see over the tops of the few trees and the thick undergrowth. Yet the track was so wide that he felt free and exposed to the sky. The wind made a sound like the sea in the treetops. It almost seemed to be alive.

He reached a place where the track turned, and on the left seemed to hang over the edge of the ridge. Far below him he saw the Black Swan, and the road they had come on looked like a thin silver band. Rolling fields faded away into a thick mist, and the farthest things he could see were a few vague pinpoints of light. The wind hovered around him, and the noise of the trees, and distant sounds that he could not identify.

He felt a drop of rain, and realized with a start that he had no idea how long he had been standing there. He turned quickly and headed back along the ridge the way he had come, thankful that he had stayed on only one path. The rain seemed to be holding back, and as he walked down the track in the fading light he felt only a few scattered drops, as though it were waiting for him to get inside. It was very dark in the thicket, and when he reached the gate he could see light in the cottage windows, and smoke coming from the chimney.

There was a blazing fire in the living room fireplace, and in the warm, dim light the room seemed comfortable. Philippa was peeling potatoes in the kitchen, which now sang with warmth and light from dozens of candles. "It's beautiful outside," he said, and at that moment the rain broke from the sky.

"Sounds as though you got back just in time," Philippa said. The rain was already rattling and hammering against all the windows, making the house seem even more warm and protecting.

"There's a wide track all the way along the ridge, and there's this one place where you can see for miles, down to the Black Swan and everything!"

"It sounds wonderful," she said vaguely.

"Is something wrong? Was I gone too long?"

"No, it's not that. It's just that—well—Islington found this . . . strange thing. I'd like you to get rid of it, please. I can't bear to touch it."

Danny followed her into the living room, imagining the rotting corpse of some small animal. "It's this," she said.

On the mantel was a small, bluntly carved wooden figure. It was hardly more than one piece of wood with a small head on it, with another piece struck through it for arms. It was very crude, and just barely suggested an expressionless human being.

"What's wrong with this?" Danny said, picking it up. "It's just something somebody whittled. It's not very pretty but it isn't hideous. Where did you find it?"

"I didn't. Islington kept prowling about near the fireplace, almost as if he had smelled something. I thought he was after a mouse. And then, he pulled that *thing* out of some crevice between the hearth and the wall. When I saw it a real shock went through me. I could hardly bear to touch it long enough to put it on the mantel. How can you hold it like that? There's something so . . . sinister and . . . menacing about it. I don't want it in the house!"

Danny fingered it and looked at it carefully. "I don't understand why you feel like that, but I don't mind getting rid of it."

He started to toss it into the fire, but Philippa grabbed his arm. "Don't!" she almost shouted. "Don't burn it up! Don't destroy it! Just take it away, take it outside." She took a deep breath. "I'm sorry to be so hysterical, but that thing really terrifies me. I don't know why."

"All right. It doesn't matter to me." He was drenched the moment he stepped out of the house. There was something wrong with the guttering, and a waterfall seemed to be pouring down just outside the door. He tramped over to the other side, planning to pitch the doll down the incline into the valley below. But he couldn't do it. There must be something remarkable about this thing if it makes her react that way, he thought, and slipped it into his coat pocket.

Inside, he took a candle and went straight upstairs. He took off his clothes and stood there for a moment, naked and shivering in the heatless room. His body was very thin and frail and covered with goose pimples. His blond hair was plastered to his head. Breathing heavily, he took the little figure out of his coat pocket and buried it in the bottom drawer of the dresser.

When he came down he was in his bathrobe and pajamas, the dripping clothes in one hand and the candle in the other. "I'll hang them up over the stove," Philippa said. "They'll dry out in no time. I'm sorry you got soaked, but I just had to have that thing out of the house."

They cooked steaks over the fire and ate them, with grilled tomatoes and boiled potatoes, at the round table by the hearth. Danny finished his steak with no prodding from Philippa, which was very rare. Somehow it did taste better than the meat they had eaten in the city, as Philippa said. He had never realized that the taste of food could be so enjoyable.

Danny helped Philippa wash up, and they spent the evening playing Scrabble in front of the fire. The rain beat down ceaselessly, occasionally sputtering into the fire. The wind moaned and rattled at the windowpanes. And although the room glowed in the firelight and the thick walls kept out the wind, neither of them felt comfortable. The back of Danny's neck tickled as though someone were watching him, and he found himself looking around frequently to the dark end of the room. Both were conscious of how isolated they were. Miles of darkness and trees, of wind and rain, separated them from any other human being.

Late in the evening Danny brought a candle up to his bedroom. On the narrow stairway a draft seemed to spring up from nowhere. The candle flickered and almost went out. Danny stopped at once and cupped his hand around the flame until it sprang back to life, his heart pounding. But why should I be so afraid? he wondered.

From his narrow bed he watched the shadows flicker dimly around the room. He tried to decide how he felt about the house. It had the kind of rustic charm that, as Philippa had said, one always imagines but rarely finds; and it was interesting to be in such a place simply because it was so unlike anything he had ever known. Yet he did not feel comfortable. Something about the house seemed to shut him out, to make him feel like an interloper. Yet at the same time he had the sensation that somehow, he was expected.

Probably everybody feels like this when they move to a new house, he told himself. But he settled down and closed his eyes without blowing out the candle.

A strange procession was winding across barren hillsides by moonlight. People in black robes chanted solemnly, monotonously, holding blazing torches above their heads. At the front of the procession were three crowned men dressed in white. The procession dragged on and on, over the same hills, with the droning, heavy chanting always

underneath. He couldn't tell whether he was in the proces-
sion, or whether he was only watching it. But all the time
he knew that something else was there, huge and dark and
menacing, lurking just beyond the torchlight, waiting
and watching.

For the first moment after he opened his eyes he heard a
woman's laughter, vague and distant. It wasn't evil, mania-
cal laughter, but free and easy, like a young girl's. He had
hardly realized it was there when it faded quickly away;
and he wondered whether he had really heard it, or if it had
just been part of the dream. The weather must have cleared,
for the room was flooded with moonlight. His candle had
gone out, and he was twisted up in the sheets. His forehead
felt cold and moist. He was afraid. The nightmare feeling
still lingered.

6

When he came down in the morning Philippa was boiling water and cooking bacon. She seemed groggy and tired. The first thing she said was, "I desperately need some more coal. Could you get me some?" He scurried off to the cellar, forcing himself not to think about being afraid. When he brought up the coal she said, "I'm afraid we need more water, too." As he strained over the pump he began to wonder, in an irritable, early-morning way, just how long he was going to be able to stand it in the country.

They ate breakfast in the dark, chilly dining room. It fit their mood. The eggs were so fresh that they tasted like a new kind of food, and the bacon was lean and thick. But they ate in silence until Philippa said, "Did you have a good night?"

"Well, not really. I had the weirdest dream. And when I woke up, part of it seemed to continue for a second. It sounded like a girl laughing."

"I had a bad night, too. I had trouble sleeping and kept waking up. Islington was restless, too. I'm so tired! And there's so much to do today. . . ."

After breakfast Danny went to look at the cellar door. There it sagged on its rusted, curling hinges, ancient and cracked. And there was the jagged, archaic list of names; all with similar dates but Mary Peachy, dateless, at the end of the list.

It was another sunny day, but they spent most of it inside, cleaning the windows, washing the floors, arranging things. Philippa decided that they had to go into town the next day. They needed candles, and more food, and perhaps an oil lamp, and maybe some whitewash. And Danny had to start studying.

Toward evening Philippa ventured outside with Danny, along the ridge. They were heavily bundled, and slogged through the mud in heavy Wellington boots. Islington loped along behind them, dashing ahead in brief spurts of energy, spinning around and gazing back at them, then stretching out on the brown turf until they caught up.

They walked together to the place where they could see the view. On the way Philippa examined almost every bush, gently turning over the leaves in her hand, and occasionally picked a spray of brown leaves, or a barren branch with an interesting shape, or a green bough from a fir tree. "Shhh!" she would say, "Listen to that bird. Is it a cuckoo? A nightjar?" Somewhere in her dim past, about which Danny knew next to nothing, she must have lived in the country, for the birdcalls, the plants, were familiar to her.

By the time they reached the overlook, Danny's arms were laden with her scratchy finds.

Philippa too was captivated by the view. Today, in the sunlight, they could see much farther. In the distance, glinting, was a smooth patch of silver-gray that they realized was the sea.

"I'd rather like to see those tumuli that Mr. Creech was talking about," Danny said. "He said they were at the other end of the ridge."

"I *do* love being outside," Philippa said, "but I don't think I could manage that long a walk. I feel like a cup of tea, and the fire. You go on, though. Just remember to start back in time to get home before it's too dark to see."

"I'll remember," he said, and carefully handed her the bundle of branches.

Beyond the overlook the track was spotted with deep ruts full of muddy water, and for a while it became very narrow, for the hillside was quite close and sloped down almost vertically into the valley. At the bottom a few cows grazed languidly among boulders and tufted grass. Beyond this place the track widened and continued as it had been before, sloping gradually upward. In the bright sunlight Danny forgot his fears of the night before and strode briskly across the brown grass, holding his arms out to feel the wind, singing at the top of his lungs until he was out of breath. He felt free and totally alone. The thought occurred to him that he could even take off his clothes, if it weren't so cold.

Eventually the track narrowed again and became a path winding through high bushes. It was impossible to stay out of the mud and he slogged through it joyfully. He fell down once or twice, and laughed out loud.

Around a bend the bushes disappeared, and he found himself at the edge of a wide plateau. This was the other end of the hill, and on either side the land sloped steeply down into two valleys. The plateau was practically level, covered with the same short brown grass, and was absolutely treeless.

At the other end were the tumuli. Although they were covered with the same grass and were gently rounded, it was obvious immediately that they were man-made. The three curving mounds were about twenty feet in height, symmetrically arranged to form the three points of a triangle. It was odd to see something so natural, like a growth on a hillside, that was so perfectly, evenly formed.

He started toward them. The wind raced across the open expanse of land, unhindered by any trees, and Danny suddenly felt chilly. He noticed that the sky was now filled with thick clouds rushing over the landscape with magical speed. On either side he could see valleys, and other hills, rolling on forever into the distance. He felt as if he could see the whole world.

As he approached the tumuli they seemed to grow taller, rising up and leaning over him. They were a bleak and desolate sight, and there was something peculiarly awesome about them. Danny remembered what Mr. Creech had said. The nearest of the mounds was just above him. He ran up, panting in the stinging air.

At the top was a little indentation which had been invisible from below. Lying in it was a girl.

"Oh!" Danny gasped, startled and out of breath, "I didn't know anybody was here."

"Hardly anyone ever comes here," the girl said calmly. She seemed to be about his own age. Her hair was tawny, shoulder-length, scattered over the grass behind her. Her face was round and very ruddy, sunburned even in winter. She had large brown eyes and a round, full mouth which looked relaxed and almost tough. She wore bluejeans and a thick, black sweater.

"The view is much prettier than I am," she said, smiling faintly. "Why don't you look at it?"

Danny turned around, embarrassed. He stared out over the misty hills, many shades of brown and green. From here he could see more of the ocean, which was dark, as though there were rain over it. But he couldn't think about the scenery; he could hardly see it. His mind was whirling with the surprise of seeing this girl here, and his ears were filled with the husky sound of her voice.

"Nice, isn't it?" she asked. "This is one of the highest places in England. And one of the most secluded. I come here quite often." Danny turned back and her eyes met his. "Are you on holiday or something?" she asked.

"No," he said. 'I live here."

"You *live* here!" For the first time she sounded surprised. "Where?"

"In this little cottage at the other end of the ridge."

"You live at *Blackbriar*? Nobody's lived there for as long as I can remember. You must have just moved in."

"Yesterday."

"Jesus!" she said. "Why don't you sit down."

As he squatted on the grass he noticed that in the center of the hollow was a ring of charred stones, as if there had been a fire there.

"How amazing that you live at Blackbriar! Even my father doesn't have the guts to live that far away from everything. What made your family decide to live there?"

"I don't have a family."

"Then who do you live with?"

"The secretary at my school. I mean, she used to be the secretary at the school I used to go to."

"No parents? My mother died when I was a baby, I just live with my father now. He's an artist."

"Do you live near here?"

"Down at the bottom of the hill, near the Black Swan. We lived in London before my mother died. I hardly remember it, but I know I couldn't bear it now."

"Philippa, that's the lady I live with, hated London too. So finally she just gave up her job and we moved out here. I didn't think I would like the country, but maybe it's going to be all right. We had no idea that Blackbriar would be so strange."

"I'll bet you didn't." She was beginning to sound calm and self-assured again. "Hardly anyone will go near the place, I don't know why. It certainly doesn't scare *me*."

"Have you ever been inside?"

"No. But sometimes I walk past it. I always wished we lived there, but my father didn't want to be so far away from the pub." She laughed. "I always look in the windows, but it's hard to see anything, they're so dusty."

"Well they aren't now, not with Philippa around. But

why *are* people afraid of Blackbriar? What do they think is wrong with it?"

"I'm not sure. Perhaps it's just kind of the local spooky place. What's it like to live there?"

"It's all right. But there is something strange about it. There's an uncomfortable feeling. I don't really understand it."

"Uncomfortable how?"

"It's hard to explain." Danny noticed with surprise that he was talking to her in a very free, relaxed way. He had always been very shy with people his own age, and since his school in London had been a boy's school, talking to a girl like this was a unique experience. But she was so forthright, and so interested, that he completely forgot to be shy. "There's a creepy feeling to the place, an atmosphere. And the basement is really frightening. It scares me to go down there, although there isn't anything obviously gruesome in it. And the door to the basement has a list of names carved on it, with dates like 1665. I can't figure out why they're there, or what the place was originally built for, so far away from everything. I mean there must have been a reason for building it."

"Nobody does seem to know why it's there," the girl said. "But I'm sure you're just afraid because it's old and dark, and you're used to living where there's crowds all around."

"That's what I would think too, except that there really *is* something frightening about it. I can feel it, but I can't explain it. It's something almost tangible."

"Well, maybe I'll see for myself some day."

They fell silent and watched the clouds roll above them, dark and threatening now. The wind was even stronger, and Danny was shivering in his heavy coat. The girl didn't seem cold at all. The ocean was no longer visible, and many of the hills were hidden in mist, so that the landscape just seemed to end abruptly.

"Do you build fires here?" Danny asked.

"No . . . You know, that could be another reason why people avoid Blackbriar, and the whole ridge." She paused, and her voice dropped dramatically, even though they could both see that there was no one within two miles of them. "Strange things go on up here. One night a few months ago I was walking down by our house, and up here on the hill I could see fires burning, big ones. And there must have been a crowd of people, because I could vaguely hear voices, as though they were singing."

Danny was immediately struck by the similarity of this story to the dream he had the night before. "Do you think what you saw might be related to that legend about the three kings buried here?"

"Perhaps," she said doubtfully.

"But on the other hand, what's so strange about having a bonfire? Maybe they were just having a picnic, and singing folk songs."

"I'm *sure* it wasn't anything so mundane. For one thing, it didn't really sound like singing. It was more like chanting. Sort of like that medieval stuff—"

"Gregorian chant?"

"Yes, but different. More . . . violent, or passionate, or something. And they were all perfectly together. That's why I could hear it. Every once in a while they would all shout. It was weird. I wanted to come up here and see what was going on, but I just didn't have the guts to do it alone."

"I wonder if it will happen again. . . ." Danny said. This is stranger than anything I ever dreamed up, he thought suddenly, and wondered if the house itself had been involved in any way. "But other people must know about it. Didn't you ask anyone?"

"They wouldn't tell me," she said bitterly.

"Mr. Creech didn't mention it to us. We *thought* his explanation sounded a bit flimsy. But if he didn't warn us about it, he must have thought it wasn't really dangerous for us to be around. I know he wouldn't tell us it was safe here if it wasn't. He just must have thought it would scare us away." He explained about the Land Rover, and how they had spent the night in the Creeches' house.

The girl lay back on the brown turf again, putting her hands behind her head. She smiled at Danny. "You know," she said, "I'm glad you've come to live here. I get pretty lonely sometimes. There aren't many other kids around this part of the country. Except for the *gentry*, of course, who are a bunch of prigs and snobs. They're always away at school anyway."

"I suppose I'm glad we've come, even though I didn't want to. I can't tell yet."

"Why did you come, if you didn't want to?"

For a moment he didn't know what to say. "Well . . . Philippa wanted me to, and she usually gets her way. And I didn't have anywhere else to live."

She looked at him strangely. "But if you really didn't want to come, why didn't you just find another—"

"Oh," he said quickly, "it doesn't matter now. I'm here."
But why *do* I let Philippa run my life? he thought. Why am
I so afraid to stand up to her? And for the first time it
seemed very wrong to him that for as long as he had lived
with her, Philippa had been practically his only companion. "Anyway, I just wish I could find out what all these
strange things mean."

"I've always wanted to find out about them too," she
said. "We can help each other."

"Yes, but *you* live down below, where there are other
people around. Philippa and I live up here in the dark,
alone." He was about to add that she also lived with her
father, someone perhaps more reassuring to have around
than a middle-aged secretary. But her confident manner,
her implication that she did not have to depend on adults,
made him feel slightly foolish. He was, after all, the man
of his house.

"Well, I'd like to come up to your house sometime," she
said. "And if there's another one of those . . . fires and
chanting things up here, we'll go together."

Danny hadn't been sure that he was going to go at all;
but now, of course, he realized he had to. It was almost as
if they had made a pact.

He felt a cold drop of rain on his forehead, and stood
up, shaking himself and stamping his feet. "I think I'd better start back," he said. "I'm not sure I could find my way
back in the dark, and I already got drenched last night."

"Yes," she said, getting up too, "I have to fix something
for my father to eat." Suddenly they were awkward.

"Oh," Danny said, "what's your name?"

"Lark," she answered, holding out her hand, "Lark Hovington."

"Mine's Danny Chilton," he said, shaking her hand. They couldn't help smiling at each other.

"Well, bye," she said, and plunged down to the plateau. When he got down, on the other side of the mound, he turned and waved. She was already starting down the hillside. "See you later!" he called, and she smiled back.

He ran almost all the way to the cottage, not because of the impending darkness and rain, but because he was happier than he could ever remember being before.

By the time he reached the house he had decided not to tell Philippa about the girl (which meant that he could not tell her the story about the fires on the plateau, either). He was afraid of what Philippa would do if he told her he had met someone he liked. In London, Philippa had successfully managed to end every friendship Danny had made. At first he had believed her explanations: it was for his own good that she did not want him to see so-and-so. But eventually it had become clear to him that she had other motives, and soon after that it dawned on him what they were. She was simply afraid to let anyone else become important in his life, for then he might be moved to leave her. She held onto him with an iron grip. When he first realized this, Danny had resented it bitterly; but, as with everything else, he had given in. She was stronger than he was. No friendship had been important enough to go through the struggle of fighting with her about it.

But now he hoped to prevent her from interfering. The only way to do so, he knew, was simply to keep Lark a secret, for he did not trust himself to stand firm against whatever objections Philippa might make.

But when she greeted him at the door Philippa was in such vivacious good spirits that he hardly had a chance to tell her he had been to the tumuli at all. Talking constantly, she led him about by the hand to see all the improvements she had made that afternoon: how the branches she had picked were arranged in pottery vases and bowls, how she had moved some of the furniture to make the room look cozier, how beautiful the wooden floors were when they were clean. The narrow kitchen was full of steam from the boiling pot of brussels sprouts, and while Philippa finished cooking the meal, Danny sat staring peacefully at the misty reflections in the window, congratulating himself on how cleverly he had managed to preserve the pleasant atmosphere that now filled the house.

Just as Philippa took the baked sausages and mushrooms out of the oven there was a short knock at the door.

"Who on earth could that be?" she asked, and banged the hot pan down on top of the stove.

"Our first visitor," said Danny. He hurried toward the door, hoping that it would not be Lark, but unable to imagine who else would be up on the ridge on a rainy winter evening. The first thing he noticed when he opened the door was the color of the sky, which had not yet become completely black. A vivid pink glow was settling down over the barren trees and fading yard, and the figure in the doorway appeared only as a darker, jagged shadow against

the mournful twilight. Two pinpoints of reflected firelight
shone from what must have been the face.

"Oh . . ." came the quiet, lisping voice, "oh, pardon me. I
was surprised to see you here." Danny peered more closely,
but the small, bright eyes were all he could see clearly.
". . . When I noticed the lights I thought it would be Mary
Peachy. But I see I was mistaken. Pardon me . . ." The figure watched him for a moment, one of its eyes twitching,
then turned away and was quickly lost in the shadows
behind.

Danny gazed briefly into the night, which was now
completely black, and slammed the door and bolted it

Philippa was clutching Islington, who, with arched back,
was hissing at the door. "What did he say?" she gasped.

Danny sat down quickly on a chair in front of the fire.
"He said . . . he thought Mary Peachy would be here!"

On the ancient door her name seemed clearer than ever
before. The only name without a date.

7

"Where's Islington?"

Lil, after a tense half hour of wheezing, dying, being pushed and cursed at, was rumbling and shaking, ready to go. The fires were out, the house was locked, blankets were piled in the front seat and baskets and empty milk bottles in the back. Philippa and Danny, sweating after their exertions in heavy clothes, stood by the rattling car.

"Where *has* he gone to, just when we're about to start?" Philippa scanned the yard and the surrounding trees. "Islington!" she called. "Islington, come here this instant!"

"I'll go hunt for him." Danny sighed, praying that the motor wouldn't die again. He started across the yard, still awkward in his heavy rubber boots. "Islington! Issssslington! Where are youuouou?" All around the house the yard was empty. Finally he walked a little way into the woods, kicking the underbrush, shouting into the trees. When he returned to the car the motor was off. Philippa was digging in her purse for the keys to the house. "I'll have to take these boots off now to go inside," she said, "and we're already so late as it is. If he's not there, I don't know what we'll do."

She unlocked the door, then leaned against the wall to pull off her boots. As he wandered around the yard Danny could hear Philippa's voice echoing faintly from inside the house. There were rustlings in the underbrush, but Islington did not emerge.

"I've found him!" Philippa called suddenly from the doorway, and Danny raced over to her. "Here, hold him while I get these bloody boots on. He was sniffing about under your chest of drawers, the nuisance! He wouldn't go near your room in London. Why he should do it here is a mystery to me." The cat stretched in Danny's arms, extending his claws. Danny felt like strangling him.

"And now this *heap* isn't going to start again," Philippa moaned, as they settled into the front seat. But, warmed up, Lil sprang immediately to life, and they creaked off down the track. As before, they lurched and scraped and bumped through the trees, always on the verge of tipping over, barely dragging through great pools of mud; but they were slightly familiar with it now and the ride was not so startling. The forest track still seemed endless though, and Islington was no more comfortable than before. This time, however, they were prepared, and heavy blankets protected Danny's legs from Islington's claws. Finally the gate appeared through the trees, and though they did tilt and bump across the field, it was a relief after the muddy track. The gravel lane that wound down the hillside was heaven.

As they descended, the dark gothic mansion on the other end of the hill came into view. Danny decided to ask Lark what kind of people lived in that gloomy place. Cows were still grazing on the green beside the Black Swan, and the warm glow in the inn windows was a welcoming sight, even after only a few days of being out of touch with the rest of the world.

As the car headed down the road to Dunchester, Danny found that he felt oddly superior to the few other drivers and the occasional cyclists. *They* just led ordinary lives, surrounded and protected by other people, policemen, gas stations, shops. But *he* lived off in the wilderness, involved with the important, natural aspects of life. He imagined himself as having just descended from a higher plane of existence to see the senseless scurryings of these trapped creatures. He was no longer caught like these others in empty routines. He was experiencing what was real.

Then he remembered the evening before, and his sense of superiority quickly disappeared. For last night he had truly begun to wonder what was real and what was not. He had hardly been able to see the strange visitor, but he could not forget that lisping voice. And what were the sinister implications of those words? Who was this Mary Peachy? Why was hers the only name without a date, and how could the stranger possibly have known her, as his words implied? He had examined the door carefully that morning and her name was clearly just as old as all the others.

Philippa pulled up beside Mr. Creech's battered gas pumps. His hair standing in the wind, his face ruddy, Mr. Creech bounced over to the car, grinning broadly. "How *is* everything?" he asked. "How do you like Blackbriar?"

"Oh, it's beautiful, Mr. Creech, beautiful," Philippa cooed. "But—"

"I *knew* you'd like it!" he interrupted. "And what about you, lad? Getting lonely up there?"

"No, Mr. Creech, it's all right," and not wanting to be interrupted, he added quickly, "especially because of all the strange things about it."

Mr. Creech seemed to be unable to think of anything to say, so Danny went on. "Mr. Creech, have you ever been inside? Do you know what those names on the door are supposed to mean?"

Mr. Creech had begun to wipe the windshield with quick, nervous strokes. "No, I never was." He stopped wiping and came around to the window. "And I wouldn't worry too much about anything strange you might see, if I was you. I told you, there's always a load of batty superstitions in an out-of-the-way place like this."

"We had a very odd visitor last night," Philippa said, and Danny could tell that she really didn't want to mention it. "He just came to the door, he didn't try to get in. But he mentioned one of the names on that door, just as if he knew the person, even though it appears to have been carved there centuries ago."

"Well," Mr. Creech said, "I can't explain the actions of everybody in this part of the country. I've told you people are superstitious about that place. You've got to expect things like that if you're going to live in such a place."

"I like things like that," Danny said almost inaudibly, not quite matching Lark's self-confident tone.

"However," Mr. Creech went on, ignoring Danny's comment, "from what you say, it sounds like it might be Lord Harleigh, of Harleigh Manor. That's the large house you must have noticed on the other side of the hill from you. He's just a harmless eccentric, likes to roam the hills at night." And that was all he seemed to want to say.

Lil was briskly filled with gas, her oil measured, her tires and water checked. "This is a damn fine wagon," Mr. Creech said. "She could make that hill four times a day with no trouble. *That* ought to make you feel comfortable up there." He stood at the gas pumps and looked after them as they rumbled away.

"Well," Philippa said, whisking the car past a small cluster of narrow stone houses, "he's a pleasant fellow, to be sure, but I still think he's not telling us everything he knows."

"But the thing is, at least he tells us something. And I do have the feeling he cares what happens to us. I mean he probably wouldn't let us stay there if it was really dangerous, don't you think?"

"Yes," she said doubtfully, "I suppose you're right."

The scattered outbuildings of Dunchester were beginning to appear around them: run-down farmhouses with tiny gardens covered with cheesecloth, a grimy pub with a tattered beer advertisement hanging over the door, garages, and sagging stucco sheds. Ahead of them was a creaking wooden cart filled with jouncing bushel baskets of cabbages, dragged by a sleepy mare who ambled along at an infuriatingly slow pace.

The road passed through a wide opening in the thick city wall. Within, the street was lined with tiny wooden shops like those Philippa had visited across from the station. The street was so narrow that although the traffic was light by London standards, it hardly moved at all, complicated by hand carts and more horse-drawn vehicles. Danny was amused by the frenetic bustle all around.

Slowly working their way through, they continued down the street until they reached the cathedral. This was a massive stone structure badly in need of repair. The entire area around the large arched entrance was covered with fantastic sculptures carved from the stone: praying, hooded women and bearded men besieged by imps and dragons and grotesque conglomerate creatures, all cut with a primitive, mournful hand. The people's mouths turned down with sorrow, their eyes looked pleadingly up to heaven in an exaggerated manner, and the creatures cackled and screamed and laughed with ferocious glee, promising even more hideous, unimaginable horrors to come.

Philippa stopped the car and for a long moment they simply stared at the façade, enchanted by the morbid complexity of the work. But at last she turned her face away. "Well," she said briskly, "I wonder where the library is. That couldn't possibly be it, right across the street there, could it?"

"Oh, yes, I guess it must be. Dreary-looking place, isn't it."

She became very businesslike. "Now, you have that curriculum from the school, don't you?" she said. "I'm sure this place will have *Julius Caesar* and *Romeo and Juliet* as well as the novels you're supposed to read. We've got your math book at home; you can work on that tonight. And we've got the *Gallic Wars*. You might try to find a Latin dictionary. And why don't you glance over the history part of that curriculum. Where are you now, the Wars of the Roses? It'll do you good to do some research and work out where you can find the information you need. I think that will probably keep you busy while I'm at the shops. And I won't be in any hurry, I feel like dawdling, maybe chatting a bit with the shopkeepers. Who knows what I might find out?"

Danny languidly trudged from the car, pausing on the library steps to watch Lil careen down the street.

The air in the library was full of dust; and the room was so dim, compared to the outside, that at first it was difficult to see anything but the round pools of light on the long wooden tables. Behind the main desk an ornate iron staircase spiraled upwards into even dimmer, dustier regions. The bald, spectacled, heavily jowled figure behind the desk turned away from his yellowed newspaper only after Danny had stood there for almost a minute. Silently, he looked Danny up and down. With great thoroughness he cleared his throat; then, his jowls swinging slowly, he asked, "Can I help you?"

"I'd . . . like to apply for a library card, sir," Danny rasped, surprised to find that his throat, too, seemed to be clogged.

"Well, I'm sure that can be arranged." The man spoke so slowly that he sounded as if he were half asleep. With a pudgy hand he pulled a faintly printed, blue-inked form from beneath the wooden surface and handed it to Danny. "If you would fill this out now, please . . ."

When Danny handed the form back, the man began to

glance at it briefly with half-closed eyes, then suddenly jerked, jiggling, out of his daze.

"What's this you say?" he asked. "Where is it you're living?"

"At Blackbriar, sir. You know, the cottage up on that hill with the tumuli, near the Black Swan."

"Yes, yes, I know the place. Who did you say you're with there?"

"I live with a secretary from the school I went to in London. I lived with her there for a long time, now we've moved out here."

"No one else there at all?"

"No, sir, no one." Why does *he* care? Danny thought. And what a strange reaction this is. He doesn't seem shocked or afraid, just a bit surprised. And much too curious.

"Well, well, well," the librarian droned, "how frightfully interesting. I wonder now," and he squinted up at Danny, "what would make two city people like you move way out to a place like that? So alone up there, nobody around to protect you, nobody to hear, if you should . . . call for help . . ."

Danny shivered in spite of himself. "We were just tired of living in the city, that's all." He was beginning to feel irritated, and even to let it show a bit in his voice. "We *like* the country, we *like* to be secluded, it's beautiful there."

"Yes, beautiful it is. So you enjoy living there, do you? Nothing . . . strange . . . about it that bothers you?"

I'm certainly not going to let *this* person know how I really feel, Danny decided. But he does seem to know about the place. Maybe if I'm clever I can find something out. "No, sir," he said, very innocently. "There isn't anything that bothers us. We both feel much better there than we ever did in London. Sometimes I feel sorry for Mary Peachy, though, with no date and all."

"What? What did you say? *Sorry* for her?" He cleared his throat several times, squinting even more intensely at Danny now. "You mean, you don't find it at all upsetting that she . . . that she . . ." Suddenly he blinked his eyes, shook his head as if gaining control of himself, and looked back at the form. "Let's see," he said, rummaging around, "I can make up a card for you right away."

"That she what?" Danny almost shouted. "That she what?"

"My dear boy," the man said sternly, "this *is* a library, you know. If this is an example of your behavior, I'm not at all sure that I should let you have a card after all."

"I'm sorry, sir," Danny whispered. "It's just that you started to say something, and I wondered what—"

"You must have misunderstood me. Now let's see, I'll just print your name here, then I sign it, then you sign it, and everything's in order. Here you are, my boy, just sign your name right on that line."

Danny signed the little beige card, almost shaking with suppressed rage and frustration. Yet he realized that if he were ever going to learn anything from this person he would have to be very subtle. And he would have to be polite.

"Now," the man said, "that chart over there explains the rules, and how the library is arranged. And over there is the card catalogue." Danny felt the dismissal, and almost forgetting to thank the man, he stepped softly across the floor. A few minutes later he glanced back from the card catalogue. A pale, willowy young fellow slouched at the desk. Danny's inquisitor was nowhere to be seen.

It didn't take him long to find the necessary books, for this was one of those libraries where one is allowed to go into the stacks. He found that he enjoyed exploring the narrow, murky avenues, and even liked the feeling of thick dust on his fingers. Many of the books had fascinating titles, and soon he forgot about everything else as he wandered among them.

Eventually, however, he began to think that Philippa might be there to meet him at any minute, and he knew she would never find him in the stacks. As he circled down toward the ground floor, his arms aching with the weight of the books, the thought occurred to him that there might be some information about Blackbriar here. He set the books down and began to search through the catalogue. Soon it began to seem useless, for though there were many books about houses, they all seemed to be concerned with famous estates or unusual architecture. The card catalogue, as stubborn as everyone else in the area, refused to yield a scrap of information.

Hopelessly he pushed in the last drawer. It was particularly frustrating to have expected to find something and then fail. He glanced around the room and noticed that the walls were lined with bound volumes of periodicals. Too dispirited to study, he started examining their titles, and discovered that most of them were local magazines or newspapers. And suddenly he was hopeful again. If there was any information about Blackbriar anywhere, the local publications were where it would be. He began poring through the indexes, worried that Philippa would arrive before he had time to discover anything.

And finally, in a crumbling and yellowed newspaper from 1935, he found what he was looking for.

8

A s she pulled away from the library, Philippa began singing happily to herself. She noticed a cartload of squealing pigs, terrified by the motion of their cart and the unfamiliar sights around them. "The darlings!" she said "Pigs you know, are even cleverer than you are, Islington, dear." She turned around in a driveway and headed back toward the main street. "How I love this town," she said softly, and laughed out loud as she fought her way through the traffic. Soon she pulled the car into a side street and parked beside a row of old brick houses.

"Lucky boy, Islington," she said as she slung her leather handbag over one shoulder. "You get to come with me today." She set the cat on her other shoulder where he sat, perfectly balanced and at ease, swaying gently as she marched off down the street, his head darting about with intense interest at all the unusual sights.

The first shop she entered was a hardware store. She bought two oil lamps, whitewash, a paraffin stove, an ax, a saw, and a hammer and nails to fix some of the loose steps. But by the time she came out of the store, buried in bundles, her feeling of well-being was gone. The man behind the counter had been very friendly until Philippa had mentioned where she lived. Then, like the others, he had made a few ambiguous remarks and refused to say another word.

Not wanting to carry Islington on her shoulder now, she looped the end of his leash around her waist. But Islington seemed to be feeling as bad tempered as Philippa, and after a few unhurried paces he stopped and sprawled out on the cobblestone sidewalk. "Oh, come *on*, darling!" Philippa said, tugging at the leash as well as she could without dropping anything. But Islington refused to move.

She sighed, shifted her bundles, and pulled on the leash again, this time more forcefully. "You certainly have been a pest today," she said. "I shouldn't have let you come with me." Islington rolled over and began licking his paw. "Will you come *on*!" Philippa almost shouted, and jerked the leash so hard that the cat was dragged a few inches along the pavement. Now even more stubborn, he lay there limply, pretending to be asleep. Philippa's bundles were beginning to slip from her aching arms.

Just as she was about to give him another tug, a plump little man with shaking jowls rushed blindly past. His foot caught on Islington's leash and, almost falling over, he slammed into Philippa, knocking most of her parcels to the ground and dragging Islington a few more inches along the pavement. For a moment he seemed terribly angry. "Madam," he said, "it is people like you, who stand idling in the center of a busy street, who . . . who . . ."

Philippa was about to interrupt with an equally furious retort when suddenly the man caught sight of Islington huddled at his feet. "Why," he said, "what a *gorgeous* Siamese!" He squatted down and began to stroke the cat passionately, Islington writhing uncomfortably under his touch. "I'm *so* sorry, madam," he said, looking up at Philippa. "I didn't realize you were leading this beautiful animal. A male, of course. What depthless eyes, what an uncanny intelligence they seem to possess!" Then, quickly darting around, he began to help Philippa gather up her bundles. Luckily the lamps had not fallen, and since the bags were strong, nothing was scattered over the pavement. When the parcels were restored, he turned again to Islington, holding the squirming, twisting head between his fat hands and staring into the cat's face.

After the man had remained in that position for just a bit too long he sighed and slowly stood up. He removed his hat, and bowing politely to Philippa, who was speechless, he said, "I must congratulate you for possessing such a fine creature, my dear lady. What spiritual qualities he has! Of course, one realizes that most Siamese have deep inner lives, but this one seems particularly sensitive, particularly open to the highest influences."

"Well," Philippa said, who had no idea what he was talking about, "I don't know about all *that*, but I must admit that he is a wonderful companion, a real boy. But he *can* be an awful pest."

"Oh, of course, of course," the man said, his jowls

quivering. "But if he weren't a pest, if he didn't have a mind of his own, of what importance would he be, after all? Cats like this are impossible to find. Why, I would give anything, anything to own such an animal. Only think of the possibilities, only think how he could be used—" He stopped suddenly, clearing his throat. "Good-bye, madam," he said, putting on his hat, "and—thank you, thank you!" He trotted off down the street, turning around several times to stare longingly back at them.

"My, my, Islington," Philippa said brightly, "you certainly seem to have an admirer, don't you?"

Islington, blinking and alert, seemed more than ready to be on his way.

They returned to the car, where Philippa left her parcels as well as Islington, his leash hooked securely around the steering wheel, while she finished her shopping. She spoke briefly to the people in the stores, and since Blackbriar was not mentioned, the conversations were all very pleasant. Eventually she pulled Lil up in front of the library, and left the car, with the motor running, in a no-parking zone.

For a moment she couldn't see Danny at all, but then she noticed his blond head bent over one of the tables. She went and stood behind him, but he was so immersed in what he was doing that he didn't notice her at all until she cleared her throat and said, "Well, well, look at the scholar here. Not going to school really seems to be doing you some good."

He started at the sound of her voice, then said, sounding strangely tense, "Oh, this isn't schoolwork, it's not what you assigned," adding quickly, "I did find all the books you wanted me to, though." There was an odd expression in his eyes, as if he weren't seeing her, or the library, but was gazing off into some other distant world.

"What is it that's so fascinating, then?" she asked. "*The South County Gazette*, October, 1935? Sounds *deadly* dull to me. What on earth could there be of possible interest in *that*? But we've got to hurry. I've left Lil in a no-parking zone and Islington's inside, and . . ." Her words faded as she noticed that his expression did not change. "My dear," she said softly, laying her hand on his shoulder, "what's wrong?"

"Oh, nothing, really," he said, wriggling his shoulder uncomfortably. His eyes were finally focused on her face. "Yes, let's get out of here. I've got to put these away. I'll hurry." He pushed back the chair and stood up.

Philippa glanced briefly around the library, and said, "I'd better go wait in the car. But do be quick, we've still got to stop at the egg lady's and I'd like to get back up the hill before dark." As she hurried away Danny put back the heavy volumes he had been using. Then, almost staggering with the weight of all the books he had withdrawn, he descended the library steps to the car.

9

Danny set the books down in the back of the car and slid in next to Philippa. He put a folded blanket over his legs and reluctantly drew Islington onto his lap.

"Have a currant bun, darling," Philippa said as they started off. "They're nice and hot."

"No thanks," Danny murmured absently.

"Oh, *do* have one, I'm sure they're very good. And you're looking rather peaked. Come on, dear."

"But I don't want one. I'm not hungry."

"After I went to all that trouble to buy them for you, you capriciously decide you're not hungry. That's what I call—"

"Oh, all right."

As soon as he had taken one from the waxed bag by his side, Philippa reached in herself, and ate a bun quickly as she drove. They went back down the main street and left the town through the same gate in the city wall. The cold winter light was beginning to die, and the countryside took on the aura of magic and melancholy that only winter twilight can give. The car seemed a very small thing in a cold, windy universe of dark orange sky and golden hills.

"I was trying to find something about Blackbriar," Danny said quietly. "That's why I was reading those newspapers."

"No wonder you were so interested! That must mean you did find something. What a relief, after all the double-talk we've been getting. I found nothing new, of course," and she described what had happened in the hardware store. "What he said made me feel as though there were something wrong with *me*, as though somehow, there was something evil about the house, and I was part of it. It was so infuriating that I couldn't bear to mention a thing to anyone else," she finished. "It would have driven me up the wall to have the same thing happen another time."

"I'm afraid the people around here just aren't going to tell us anything," Danny said, and told her what the librarian had said.

"Mmmm," said Philippa, "but when are you going to tell me what you found out? Does it make any sense of all this?"

"It sort of does. I mean, it begins to explain it in a way. It was just a little article, about what Blackbriar used to be used for . . ."

"Well? Come on, darling, stop mumbling. What was it? Are you afraid to tell me?"

"No! It's just kind of surprising, that's all. It's just that . . . well . . . Blackbriar was a pesthouse."

The car came to a gravelly halt. They had stopped at the egg lady's gate. Philippa switched off the motor and suddenly they could hear the wind, making dry, creaking noises in the trees. "A pesthouse?" Philippa said. "Can't you be more specific?"

"Oh, yes," he said, "the article was very clear, as far as it went." The wind was streaming into every crack and crevice in the car and he could hardly keep from shivering. "The article was about the oldest building around here, and they weren't really sure whether Blackbriar was or not. But the earliest records they have of it were from the time of the Great Plague, you know, the bubonic plague, when it hit England in 1665. Blackbriar was where they put away the people from Dunchester who caught it."

Philippa was gazing at him silently, her lips slightly parted. Now that he had broken the ice, he went on quite rapidly. "I did some research on the plague today. The first time it came, three quarters of the population of Europe died from it. It sounds like such an awful disease, with people getting huge sores on their bodies that itched and stung and were so painful that people would just scream and writhe around uncontrollably. And they had fits and convulsions too. I think it affected the brain, people would go mad from the pain and run around helplessly, not knowing where they were or what they were doing, trying to rip the swellings from their flesh. . . . That explains the names on the door, of course. All those people died there, from the plague. I still wonder about Mary Peachy, though, why she had no date. I was thinking, maybe she was the last one to die, and there was nobody left to put it down."

For a moment Philippa was silent. Then, her voice

husky, she said, "I'll go get the milk and eggs," and dashed from the car.

Truly shivering, Danny absentmindedly pulled Islington more tightly against him. Oddly enough there was something comforting about stroking his warm, gently breathing body. He wondered vaguely why Islington did not protest, but soon began to think about what that strange man had said the night before. Mr. Creech had told them he was a harmless eccentric, and maybe his words were nothing but confused, meaningless prattle. But there was something about the way he had said them that made it difficult for Danny to get them out of his mind. There must have been something very special about Mary Peachy for the man to speak of her like that, something more than just being the last to die. The librarian, too, had reacted to her name. But what was there about her? And what could last night's visitor possibly have meant by suggesting that she might be there? It was clearly impossible that she could still be alive. Yet that was what the words had implied, and Danny could not forget them.

Soon Philippa returned, and with brisk movements tightly packed the milk bottles, egg cartons, and a pot of fresh butter into the back. Roughly, she jerked the car away, and soon they were driving through the little forest with the gnarled roots. Here it was almost night, the thick, twisted shadows of the trees stretching out across the road. "Well," Philippa said at last, "that certainly is a piece of information. But I'm not sure how grateful to you I am for finding it out, I must say."

"But you know we'd have had to find out sometime. We were just too curious not to."

"Yes, I suppose so. But tell me, how do you feel about living there now?"

"I don't really know. I suppose it's silly to worry about the place still being infected; it couldn't be, after all those years, and nobody gets the plague now anyway. But I'm sure that really isn't what's bothering either of us. It's just the idea of it, that all those people died such horrible deaths there. I mean, that's the only frightening thing. And why should that have any effect on us, really? I mean, unless we believed in ghosts or something, which we don't."

"Yes, yes, I know all that. But, I just don't know if I can bear the continual thought that right in my own bed, right where I'm sleeping, somebody was rotting away in mindless agony." For a moment she closed her eyes and shook her head back and forth, then quickly snapped her attention back to the road. "I'm sorry," she said, "I'm an emotional person. I'm even a bit superstitious. And I know that something like this can work its way into my head and just dominate all my thoughts. I just don't know, I don't know."

Well, Danny thought, now it's going to be easy to persuade her to leave this uncomfortable place and go back to London. Briefly he pictured the London apartment, and the kind of life he had had there. And he realized, with a shock, that he really didn't want to go back. "But haven't you grown to like the house?" he asked. "In the few days we've been there I've really got used to it. I know we felt uncomfortable at first; but actually, that probably *was* that we just weren't used to being isolated. Now that you've fixed it up and made it so cozy and nice, why, it almost seems to me that there's something benevolent about the place."

Philippa glanced at him suspiciously. "But *you're* the one who didn't want to come here in the first place. What's made you change your mind? Good God, there's still so much we don't know about the place! Why was that awful wooden figure there, for instance? No, I'm sure this isn't the complete answer. I'm sure we've only tapped the surface. It would take more than this plague business to make everyone hate Blackbriar so much."

"But that's another reason why I want to stay. I've got to find out the rest of the story."

Philippa flipped on the headlights, murmuring, "Now we'll have to drive up there in the dark." They drove on in silence until they reached the Black Swan. She pulled into the driveway. "I'm going in for a drink," she said. "You can come in with me if you want."

10

It was dark inside the public house, and hot, and the air hung with smoke. There was the heavy pub smell of rich beer and cigars, and the hum of glasses and conversation. Behind the stained mahogany bar, bottles of every size and shape were arranged in pyramids against dark wooden columns and oval mirrors reflecting a darker, smokier room. The heavy beams on the ceiling were hardly discernible, and the fire blazing in the stone fireplace, which was big enough for a man to walk into, flickered over the groups of people huddled around the bar, standing in corners, seated on black leather window seats or at the round wooden tables scattered about the room.

They made their way to the bar. Danny felt slightly uncomfortable, never having been in such a place before, but the bearded bartender hardly seemed to notice him at all. "What'll it be, madam?" he asked Philippa, wiping off the counter with a white cloth.

"Gin and French, please," she said, "but only a *drop* of French."

"And for you, my lad? A ginger beer? A lemonade?"

"Some lemonade, please."

Philippa paid for the drinks, and they made their way to a table in the corner near the fireplace, where no one would be able to hear them. The tabletop was comfortably scarred and stained, and there was a large black ashtray in the center. Philippa took a sip of her drink and lit a cigarette. "We can't stay long," she said. "I'll just have this one drink. But I do need something to help me face that place now." She took a nervous puff and stared into the fire.

His elbows on his knees, his chin in his hands, Danny studied her face. In the firelight it looked soft and worn, the skin loose, her eyelids drooping in a way that was weary rather than just tired. He wondered if it was wise to have told her what he had learned about Blackbriar.

She took another slow sip, and a long column of ash fell from her cigarette onto the floor. "If we leave here," she said, "we'll have nowhere else to go, nowhere."

Danny sat up so quickly he almost knocked over his chair. He hardly had time to be amazed at his own concern as he leaned toward her across the table and said in an intense whisper, "Leave here? But why? Just because it was a pesthouse once a million years ago? Just because some people died there? People die everyplace. People had the plague everywhere! How can you mean it?" He had never argued with her so vehemently before; until now, he had never cared enough about anything.

"I hardly know what I mean," she said slowly. "I can't bear the thought of moving again, I can't bear the thought of looking for another place to live. But I wonder if I can bear to go on living there. . . ."

"But—" Danny sighed and fell loosely back into his chair. How could she be so stodgy and unadventurous? He searched his brain for something nasty to say to her.

But before he had a chance to say anything he felt a light tap on his shoulder, and turned to find Lark standing behind him. "Oh, hullo," he said, getting up awkwardly. "I was wondering if you would be here." She was still wearing jeans and the thick black sweater, and her hair was no neater than it had been the day before on the windy hillside.

"I didn't expect *you* to be," she said. "Why should anybody be in this place when they could be up there with just the wind and the trees all around, in your wonderful house? Well, aren't you going to introduce me?"

"Oh," he said. "Right. Philippa, this is Lark. I met her at the tumuli yesterday. And this is Mrs. Sibley, the lady I live with."

"Hello," Philippa said. She turned to Danny. "You didn't tell me you'd met anybody yesterday."

"I—I guess there just wasn't time," Danny said lamely, trying to hide his embarrassment. "I mean, so many other things happened last night that—"

"I'm very glad to meet you," Lark interrupted, somewhat timidly, Danny noted.

"Why don't you sit down," Philippa said coldly. "Danny, pull up a chair for her."

He was ashamed to be told what to do in front of his independent friend; but there was nothing he could do but pull back a chair and then flop carelessly back into his.

"I've been wanting to meet you ever since I met Danny," Lark began, leaning forward. "I knew I would like anybody who liked Blackbriar, especially someone who would come all the way from London to live there."

"You might not like her, then," Danny said. "She wants to leave."

"Oh, come now," Philippa said. "You're exaggerating, and you're not telling the whole story. The truth is," she went on, turning to Lark, "that I have been wondering, just wondering, if we really should go on living there. You must know the strange attitude people have about the place. They seem either disgusted or afraid, and so secretive, all of which does have some relevance, after all. And now it turns out that Blackbriar has a really rather macabre history, as Danny discovered today."

"What did you find out?" Lark asked quickly.

"Oh, it was a pesthouse," Danny said, trying to make it sound boring and ordinary. "When the Great Plague came in the seventeenth century that's where they put the people from Dunchester who caught it. I told you about that door, remember? All the names on it must be the people who died there."

Lark gave a long, low whistle and slowly leaned back in her chair. "I see what you mean," she said to Philippa. "That's about as ghastly as you can get." To Danny she said, "How clever of you to find that out! And in less than a week as well. I've been here for practically as long as I can remember, and I had no idea it had been used for that."

Danny felt a quick wave of pleasure. It was the first time he had ever been complimented for something he had done completely on his own, perhaps because he had never really done anything on his own before.

"Yes, yes," Philippa said. There was an unpleasant edge to her voice. "I'm sure we all appreciate how very clever Danny is. But I don't understand why no one will tell us anything about the place."

While Lark was explaining to Philippa that the people in this part of the country were really quite secretive, Danny suddenly remembered that he hadn't told her not to mention the chanting on the tumuli to Philippa. Now she was probably going to say something about it, and Philippa would be furious that he hadn't told her, as well as even more convinced that they shouldn't stay. Every time Lark opened her mouth Danny was sure her next words would give it away. Silently he begged her not to mention it, while he desperately tried to think of some way to keep her quiet without making Philippa suspicious.

But in a moment Philippa finished her drink and stood up. "I'm going to the loo," she said. "And then we've really got to get back. There's the firewood to find, the oven to light, the lamps to fill, the dinner to cook, poor Islington's been cooped up in that car practically all day . . ." And she moved off into the smoke.

Danny breathed deeply. "I kept thinking you were going to tell her about all those people at the tumuli!"

"Oh, didn't you tell her? But you shouldn't have worried.

I got the drift of what was going on. She seemed to be on the *verge* of wanting to leave, so it would have been stupid of me to remind her of something like that, even if she already knew. I suppose it was wise of you not to tell her."

"It certainly seems that way now. But listen, there's this thing I forgot to tell you the other day." And he described the doll, told about Philippa's reaction to it and how he had secretly hidden it in his room.

"I'm dying to go up there now," Lark said. "I can't wait to see all these things you've been telling me about. I wonder if it would be possible . . ."

"I can ask her," Danny said, and then added quickly, "and anyway, it's my house too. She has no right to refuse—"

Lark motioned to him to be quiet, for Philippa was approaching the table. They both looked up guiltily, but she seemed too preoccupied to notice. Quickly Danny said, "Philippa, could Lark come back to the house with us now?"

Philippa looked at Lark doubtfully. "Well, you'd have to spend the night. I'm not driving back down again, you know. If you think your father would approve . . ."

"I'm sure he would."

"Well, in that case, I suppose it's all right."

"Oh, thank you so much! That's *super.* I've just got to go and tell my father. I mean ask."

"And you must be sure to tell him precisely where it is we live," Philippa said, as the three of them started for the door, "in case he has any objections to your spending the night in that house."

"Oh, I'm sure he won't worry about it."

Danny pulled open the heavy, iron-studded door, and

they stepped out into the starry night. The air was icy, as clear and brittle as glass. "We just live a few yards from here," Lark said. "I'll be back in a minute." She dashed off into the darkness.

"Whew! It does feel good to be able to breathe again, after being in that smoky hole for so long."

"It's a nice pub," Philippa said, climbing into the car. "You didn't have to come in, you know. And you might as well stop sulking and whining. It's not going to do any good. And besides, I was just thinking aloud. I still don't understand why you've suddenly decided to like being here—although perhaps I do now," she added slowly, looking back for a moment in the direction Lark had gone. She paused, then went on quickly. "But be that as it may, I haven't decided to leave—yet."

Danny was eager to turn the conversation away from Lark. "It would be nice if there was a heater in this thing," he said, as she started the car and turned on the lights.

"Oh, *do* shut up, will you? It's going to be hard enough to get up there in the pitch darkness as it is, without your nasty little comments. Not that I expect you to behave so childishly in front of your friend. Which reminds me, I think you'd better get in the back so that there'll be room for her. And you can keep a grip on the lamps and things so that they won't get broken on the way up."

Sighing audibly, but leaving the blanket on the front seat, Danny climbed into the back. He tried to arrange himself in a comfortable position but found that the back was full of hard edges and sharp places that stuck into him painfully. "She can take care of Islington," he said. "She has the blanket, and I'll have to be holding on to all this stuff back here."

They heard quick footsteps on the gravel, and in a moment Lark poked her head through the front window. "This must be the right car," she said brightly as she climbed in. "I *adore* Land Rovers."

"Would you hold Islington?" Philippa said. "Here, put this blanket on your lap first, he gets a bit panicky on the track and hangs on to people's legs with his claws, as I'm sure Danny will be glad to describe to you in gory detail."

"Great fun back there, isn't it," Lark said to him, turning around in her seat.

"Mmmm," said Danny.

"What was your father's reaction when you asked him about spending the night at Blackbriar?" Philippa asked as she turned onto the dirt lane that wound up the hill. "I assume he said yes."

"He did. I'd already told him about meeting Danny at the tumuli, so he knew I knew the people who were living there. He didn't say much, just told me not to get into any mischief. He did ask me what you were like, but when I told him you had been a school secretary he seemed satisfied."

"Hmph!" Philippa said. "Secretaries *can* be quite wild, you know." The engine groaned and she shifted with a lurch into a lower gear.

On the field, the moonlight was almost as bright as day. The car swayed across the open expanse of land like a small boat rocking on a silver-green sea. The night sky shimmered above them, more huge and endless than in day; but the other hilltops, like mysterious black-crowned islands, seemed to enclose them in their own lonely world, cutting them off from all that was comforting and ordinary down below. They were all eager, Danny felt, to get to the relative security of the house.

But when they reached the house and saw the firelight flickering in the windows, the pale, moonlit smoke curling from the chimney, Islington was the only one who seemed to want to get out of the car.

11

"Well," Philippa said finally, a slight tremor in her voice, "the perfect end to this wonderful day. Now what do we do?"

Islington scratched at the door, eager to begin his nightly mouse hunt around the yard.

"You're sure you didn't leave a fire burning this morning?" Lark asked.

"I would never leave a fire burning in an empty house. And even if I had, it would have burned out hours ago."

For a moment no one spoke. Then, turning to face Danny (who was waiting for her to decide what to do), Philippa said, "Well? I thought you wanted to find out all about this place. Didn't I hear you make some remark about how ridiculous it was to be afraid?"

"What I said was . . ." Danny began, and then stopped. They were both staring at him. What would Lark think of him if he didn't do something? He sighed. "Well," he said peevishly, "how can I get out of the car unless somebody moves?"

Lark opened the door and Islington sprang through it, disappearing immediately into some bushes. Lark stepped out cautiously, and Danny followed her.

"What are you going to do, then?" Philippa whispered.

"Just . . . I don't know. Look in the windows, I suppose."

"I'll wait for you here. And you two had better be careful."

Danny started quietly across the yard, Lark close behind him. He felt helpless and exposed, and every step was an effort. But he hated to think of what Philippa would say if he backed down, especially in front of Lark; and somehow he was able to put each foot forward mechanically, trying not to think what he might find.

Finally he reached the house. Holding his breath, he peered through one of the living room windows.

The fire, which looked freshly built, only dimly illuminated the room. But although there were some dark corners, Danny was sure no one was there. "Let's look through the other windows," he whispered. They slunk around to the other side, and from this viewpoint the room seemed as empty as before. Silently, they peered through the other ground-floor windows. All the rooms were empty.

"But there could still be somebody upstairs," Lark whispered, as they started back to the car. "And if anybody is there, they'll know we're back. That car makes an awful lot of noise in the quiet up here."

"Well?" Philippa said, leaning out of the car window, "well?"

"Nothing," said Danny.

"Nobody," said Lark.

"Then the only thing we can do now is go inside," Philippa said. Do we have to? Danny almost whined, but stopped himself in time. Philippa twisted around and struggled with the packages in the back of the car, finally unearthing a huge flashlight. "We can use this as a weapon as well as a light source," she said, stepping out of the car and then smoothing her skirt nervously. "Shall we get started, then?"

The key in the lock seemed to make an incredible amount of noise, and Danny was sure the door had never squeaked so loudly. Philippa switched on the flashlight. Its yellow beam darted into all the corners, exposing no crouching figures. "Shhhh!" she hissed as she led them into the kitchen. "Be as quiet as possible so we can hear any other noises there might be."

Danny hung behind her nervously. He thought of their conversation in the car, and wondered why he had spoken so bravely, without really thinking about how frightening the house could be. He also wondered what he would have done in the present situation if Philippa had not been there. All at once the London apartment did not seem so bad.

The kitchen was untouched, not a dish or a towel out of place. The dining room table was still covered with the crumbs Danny had forgotten to wipe away after breakfast, and as they approached the door to the stairway Philippa managed to shoot him an annoyed glance.

She pulled open the door as slowly and silently as she could, then paused for a long moment, listening. There were creaks, and something that sounded like scratching, but it was hard to tell in an old house which noises were natural and which were not. Finally she started up the stairs, flinging the beam ahead of her. Lark and Danny were just behind.

Danny's bedroom was empty. As they stepped into the middle room Philippa whispered to Lark, "This is where you'll be sleeping." This room was empty too. Philippa's bedroom was the largest and most shadowy. Hardly cautious anymore, she flashed the light around her. "Naturally, no one would be under the bed," she said, and they all peered into the cavern beneath the sagging mattress.

There was a quick scuffling behind them. Philippa spun around the light. Suddenly Lark and Danny were clutching each other.

Islington was pawing about in the ashes of the fireplace. "Oh, you monster!" Danny cried. His knees were shaking.

"Don't you talk to him like that!" Philippa said angrily. "He can't help it, he's just playing." She kneeled down. "Come here, darling." Islington curled and stretched under her hand.

"Well, now I suppose we've got to look in the basement," Danny muttered.

"Yes," Philippa said, standing up. "Come on, let's get it over with."

It was Philippa who led the way down the basement steps. Danny did not stay very close behind her, until Lark stepped on his heel in the darkness and automatically he moved forward quickly. He had never been in the basement with Philippa before, and found that the room was not necessarily as frightening as he had thought.

"It really is creepy down here," Lark whispered.

Philippa flashed the light over the damp stone walls. "There certainly isn't anyone here," she said at last.

There was a short silence.

"But what's going on?" Danny said suddenly. "And who would build that fire, and why?" Now that it was clear that they were the only people in the house, his courage very quickly returned. "We have to find out. I mean, we can't let people come in and out of here without trying to find out who it is, and why they would do it!"

"Listen," Philippa said, "what we really have to do is get organized. We can't just stand here all night blathering and dithering. We've got to keep busy, and try to think about something else for a while. Why don't you two unload the car while I get the stove going. Then, Lark, you can fill the lamps and the paraffin stove, I'm sure you know how, and Danny can do some pumping, and I'll start dinner and get Lark's bed made up. Then, when we have light, and some food in our stomachs, we'll be able to think much better about what we should do."

Lark and Danny brought the small flashlight out to the car. Danny tried to think of something to say that would show Lark how calm he was. "Philippa is a wonderful cook," he finally managed, as they began to gather up the food and the equipment in the back of the car.

"That's too bad. I love to eat, and it's a real treat for me to eat someone else's cooking. But I don't have much appetite now. I'm still nervous about that fire."

"I can't imagine why anyone would have built it."

They put the bundles down in the kitchen, where Philippa was poking around in the oven with the big flashlight. "This is going to take some time," she said when she emerged. "It's hard enough to get this monster started in daylight. Lark, do you know how to deal with these lamps?"

"Well, sort of. You just fill them with paraffin, and I know how to pump and light this hurricane one. But this other thing, the Aladdin lamp, you have to put this asbestos filament in, or something, and I don't know how to light it."

"Just do the hurricane and fill the Aladdin. I think you'd better do it outside, if you don't mind. I don't want paraffin all over the floor. Do it on that old table out there."

Outside the door was a large round wooden table, gray and mottled with long years of continuous exposure to every kind of weather. Lark brought out the flashlight and set down the two lamps and the little stove, then meticulously began to pour paraffin into them from a large metal can.

Danny was on the cellar landing, beginning to pump. The first few strokes were a struggle, but soon he developed a rhythm which made it somewhat easier. The surprise of what had just happened had filled him with nervous energy; and his thoughts were spinning so fast that he practically forgot he was pumping at all. Somewhere in the back of his mind, however, he continued to count the strokes. He pumped till his arms ached and he felt stiflingly hot in his heavy coat. And after he had taken it off, dropping it carelessly on the stone floor, he began to pump again, hardly knowing what he was doing. Finally his arms simply refused to move, and when he stopped he noticed that his shirt was wet through, and sweat was dripping down his forehead and rolling off his cheeks. He had never really sweated before in his life, and was quite surprised that he was capable of it. As he wobbled up the steps on shaking legs, panting heavily, he realized that he had done seventy strokes, more than twice as many as he had been able to do before.

"You were certainly down there a long time," Philippa said as he came into the kitchen. She was spreading out the glowing coals at the bottom of the stove with an iron poker.

"I know," he gasped. "I did seventy strokes! The most I could do before was thirty."

There was a sudden hissing noise from outside, then a brilliant glow, wavering at first, but soon steady. Lark walked into the kitchen, proudly holding the hurricane lamp above her head.

"How marvelous!" Philippa cried, clapping her hands together. "At last I can *see*! Now I can really begin to cook again. Danny, hang the lamp on that hook over the stove."

He scraped an old wooden rocking chair from a corner, balanced on it, swaying, and slipped the shiny metal handle of the lamp over the blackened hook sticking out of the wall. He jumped down and surveyed the kitchen as he dragged back the chair. It was like a different room, bright and cheerful now, larger than the dim, cramped space it had been before.

"Thank you so much," Philippa said to Lark. "It changes my whole state of mind to have a decent place to cook."

Danny went upstairs to make Lark's bed, and Lark brought in the Aladdin lamp and the little stove. She and Philippa began preparing the food.

Philippa didn't seem very eager to talk to Lark, and they worked in silence until finally Lark said, hesitantly, "You really are lucky to be living here, you know."

"Yes, it's really too bad about this place," Philippa said, sticking little slices of garlic into a large hunk of red meat. "I mean, it would be such a divine place to live if it weren't for this mysterious business. And I had thought that it would be good for Danny to live in a place like this. He's hardly ever been in the country in his life."

"I'm sure it will be good for him," Lark said eagerly, scraping the last bit of peel off her second potato. She chopped it in half and dropped it into a saucepan filled with water, then quickly started on another. "He's quite skinny and pale; kids need to live where they can be outdoors. *I* think it's terribly unhealthy to grow up in the city. My father is always saying how much better it is to live here than in London. He says it's much easier to concentrate and work hard, and that his paintings have more to them than the ones he did in London."

"Oh, so your father's a painter, is he?" Philippa sounded bored, as if she were making an effort to think of something to say. "What are his paintings like?"

"Oh, I don't know, they're hard to describe. They're abstractions . . . I guess I don't understand them." There was another silence. "But sometimes he does sketches of people," Lark said quickly, obviously making an effort to keep the conversation going, "like some of the old men in the tavern, and those are wonderful. They're really alive." She put down the knife and the potato and began gesturing with both hands. "And they look just like the people they're supposed to be. But the great thing about them is that they also show what my father thinks of the person, and what his personality is like." She began peeling again, then smiled to herself. "Sometimes we have arguments about them, because he has different feelings about people than I do. I mean sometimes he'll show somebody looking kind of sly, who I think is just thoughtful, or he'll make somebody look dumb and gossipy who really just likes to talk. And I always say, 'But so-and-so isn't *like* that,' and he just says, 'My pen never lies,' or something else grand and pompous. He's just teasing then, but I really think he does have a kind of black view of most people. Sometimes I wonder if he's a . . . what's the word?"

"Misanthrope, do you mean?"

"Yes, I guess so."

"Hmmm," Philippa said. She set the meat into a large roasting pan and, grunting genteelly, slid it into the oven. "I'm just guessing about how hot this oven is," she went on. "It seems slow enough for the meat to be juicy and rare, but I'm going to have to remember to keep checking it. Now, how are the potatoes coming?"

"I've just finished them. You're sure this isn't going to be too much? Ten potatoes is a lot for three people."

"Oh, no, that certainly isn't too much. In fact, I wonder if it's going to be enough. I adore potatoes myself, and Danny likes them too, and I'm sure you have a healthy appetite. Potatoes are very good for you, you know, full of vitamins and minerals, make you laugh and play. And they really aren't fattening at all."

"That's funny, I always thought they *were* fattening."

"A common misconception. Anyway, we won't start cooking them for a while, salad and vegetables can start later too, after the meat's been cooking. Timing things with all this primitive equipment just may drive me up the wall. Now, dessert . . . Are you very hungry?"

Lark was about to say no, for she was still slightly shaky. But just at that moment she noticed the smell of the beef and garlic beginning to cook, and realized that she was absolutely starving. Her stomach felt so empty that there seemed to be nothing at all between her shoulders and legs. "As a matter of fact, I am quite hungry," she said.

"Apple pie," said Philippa. "Now that there's light I can make pastry quite easily here."

"Oh, I don't want to make you go to all that extra trouble."

"No trouble, no trouble."

"You've got to let me help you, then."

"The one thing I'm going to ask of you is to please stay out of the kitchen. Making puff pastry takes great concentration and I must not be disturbed. So just go and scamper off somewhere. I'll let you know when I need you."

Lark lit a candle while Philippa began measuring out the flour, and walked up the stairs to Danny's bedroom. As she came up he was hastily shutting one of the bureau drawers.

"I didn't really think you were Philippa," he said, turning around. "You have a lighter step. But I didn't want to take any chances." He opened the drawer again and took something out. "This is the doll I was telling you about."

She set down her candle next to his and sat beside him

on the narrow bed. He handed her the strange wooden figure. She examined it slowly and carefully.

"This really looks ancient," she said softly. She turned to look at him. Their faces were very close. "And you say that Philippa . . . reacted how?"

He moved away from her slightly. "She practically got hysterical. She couldn't bear to touch it. What was it she said? That it was sinister, and menacing, or something."

"And she insisted that you get rid of it?"

"Yes, but she wouldn't let me burn it. I was supposed to throw it down the hill."

"How odd. I wonder why she did that. I wonder what it really is." Lark handed it back. Somehow she had managed to slide close to him again.

Danny stood up quickly and put the doll back in the drawer. He did not return to the bed, but stood and looked out the window. It was small, and there was a little square space almost a foot thick between the inside wall and the glass. He gazed blankly out at the trees and sky. A stream of icy air blew across his face, for though the window was closed as tightly as possible, the wind still managed to get through. There was no heat at all in the room, but the fire downstairs and the thick walls kept it from being quite as cold as one would expect.

Finally he turned around. "Something really smells delicious," he said. "What's she making?"

"Roast beef. And apple pie."

"She makes fantastic apple pie. God, I'm hungry. I've *never* been this hungry before. Why don't we go down where we can smell it better."

"If you want."

"Let's go, then," he said quickly, starting for the stairway. "And you haven't even seen the door yet, have you?"

"What door?" She remained on the bed.

"You know, the door with all the names on it. How come you're so funny all of a sudden?"

She stood up quickly. "I'm not being funny. And you better not go down that way. She said she didn't want anybody in the kitchen."

"Well have to go through her bedroom then."

Each holding a candle, they walked through the two other bedrooms and down the stairs. The stairway was only wide enough for one person, and so steep that you had to concentrate to keep from plunging down head first. The steps were well-worn dark wood and made a 180-degree turn, so that each step was triangular, one side too small to step on. The walls here, as everywhere else in the house, were nubbly and whitewashed, and formed an oddly shaped, twisting passageway beneath the sloping ceiling. The candlelight made hovering patterns around them as they descended.

"Please," Philippa called from the kitchen as soon as Danny stepped down into the living room, "I don't like people trampling through my room all the time. There *is* another stairway, you know."

She's really in a rotten mood, Danny thought. He looked at Lark, sighing. "But I thought you didn't want us in the kitchen," he called, "so we had to come down that way."

"What are you mumbling about?"

"Oh, nothing, forget it." He motioned to Lark to come over to the door. "Here it is," he said, holding up the candle.

Lark examined the door, running her finger along the grooves in the wood. It was very smooth, almost shiny. "This is really incredible," she said at last. "Just imagine— all these people dying here. But it does seem strange that they would have the strength or the will power to keep this record. I mean, you'd think that they'd be in such pain they wouldn't even think about doing this."

"Do you notice anything else about the writing?"

Lark looked again carefully, then stepped back for a moment. "Actually, all the writing looks the same. It looks like the same person did it all. Is that what you mean?"

"Yes. I wanted to see if you thought so too. And you know what it makes me think?"

"What?"

"That Mary Peachy must have done it. She wrote it down whenever anybody else died. And she must have been the last one to die, because there was no one to put the date after her name. Can you imagine it? To have everybody dropping dead all around you, and then to be left all alone, just waiting to die?"

"I wonder what happened to all the bodies. I wonder if she had to bury them herself."

"I wonder what happened to *her* body," Danny whispered. Almost uncontrollably, a twisted smile crept across his face.

Lark grabbed his arm. "What's wrong with you? How can you smile like that?"

"Oh, I'm not really smiling. It's just that . . . it's all too much. It's so impossibly creepy. I mean her body could very well still *be* here, just left to rot away over the centuries."

Lark thought for a moment. "I wonder if that doll in your room has—"

"Shhh! I'm not supposed to have it, remember?" He looked toward the kitchen. "Try not to talk so loud."

"But I wonder how it fits in," she whispered. She looked again at the door. "You know, Mary Peachy couldn't have been very sick if she had the strength to carve all those names, and take care of all those bodies. She really sounds like she must have been a remarkable person, awfully brave and independent. That's how I've always wanted to be."

"Yes," Danny murmured. "Brave and independent . . . I suppose that's the way to be." Suddenly he felt tired, and strangely sad. Ignoring Lark, who, bewildered by his sudden change in mood, still stood by the door, he sat down slowly in one of the chairs and gazed silently into the fire.

Brave and independent, he thought. And I'm so cowardly and weak. Why didn't I ever think of it before? Why didn't I ever care about it before? And is there anything on earth that could ever make me any different?

12

Dinner that night, as Danny had expected, was not the pleasantest of meals.

Just before they had sat down to the onion soup in its little covered bowls, Philippa had burned her hand lighting the Aladdin lamp. Though the lamp now glowed gracefully in the center of the table, Philippa's hand was encased in awkward cloth bandages, and her face, Danny noted with dismay, showed all the signs of a terrible mood.

"Cheese?" Philippa said in her iciest, most polite voice.

"Thank you." Lark uncovered her bowl, sprinkled cheese on her soup, then passed it to Danny. They waited while Philippa very slowly took cheese herself, gazed off into the distance for a long moment, and at last picked up her spoon. They began to eat.

"Why, this is *delicious*," Lark said. "It's the best onion soup I've ever had."

"Oh?" said Philippa.

"It *is* good," Danny said. "Tonight it's even better than usual."

"Oh, so you don't like it the way I usually make it, do you?"

Danny sighed. "That's not what I meant," he said.

They finished the soup in silence. The lamplight fell across the polished wood, the green bowls, the heavy silver, their hands, and up into their faces; but outside the circle of the tabletop the boundaries of the room were lost in darkness. Danny had the uneasy sensation that they were suspended in black, empty space with only the yellow lamplight keeping them from floating off, far away from each other.

"I'll take the bowls out to the kitchen," Lark said, sliding her chair back. "Your hand . . ."

"You won't know where to put them, though."

"I'll help her," Danny said. In the kitchen they exchanged worried looks as they stacked the dishes in the sink. Under Philippa's direction they brought the crusty roast to the table, on a wooden carving board, the Yorkshire pudding (which had puffed beautifully), the boiled potatoes, and the parsnips. With difficulty, because of the bandages, Philippa began to carve thin slices of beef, dark brown on the outside, pink and bloody in the middle.

"Well," said Philippa, as she handed Lark a large, heavy plate piled high with everything, "why don't the two of you tell me what you were whispering about while I was in the kitchen."

Lark put down her plate and stared silently at the great steaming mound of potatoes. Danny played with his fork.

"Well?" Philippa said. She passed Danny a plate with even more food on it, and fixed him with a penetrating stare.

Danny set the plate in front of him. How am I going to eat all this? he thought "Nothing," he said. "We weren't whispering."

"Oh, come now," Philippa said. "Next you'll be telling me it was Islington. The gall! There I am, slaving away in the kitchen, making an apple pie for you that I don't even want, and you're lazing about by the fire, telling secrets. It's infuriating!" She sighed angrily, and finished serving herself.

As she picked up her knife and fork she turned to Lark. "We'll drop this for now," she said. "I don't want to embarrass our *guest* with a family squabble. But," she said to Danny, "I'll worm it out of you sometime, no doubt. I've always been able to before."

They all ate rapidly. Danny noticed that the food on Lark's plate was disappearing just as quickly as his or Philippa's. It would have been difficult for anyone to eat slowly, the food was all so delicious. The meat was juicy and rare, with a slight hint of garlic; the pudding was crusty on the outside, moist and greasy in the middle; the parsnips were tender and vaguely sweet; and the potatoes, though they were served plain and boiled, with nothing but salt and pepper, were nevertheless tasty and satisfying.

"More?" Philippa said.

"Just a bit of meat, please," said Lark, lifting her plate. "It's so good."

"More meat?" Philippa sounded shocked. "My dear girl, this meat has to last us for the next three days. We're not rolling in wealth, you know. Have some more potatoes."

"Oh, no thank you. I'm really not—"

"Nonsense," Philippa said, picking up Lark's plate herself and piling potatoes onto it. "Potatoes are very good for you. Full of vitamins and minerals, make you laugh and play. And here," she added, "I think I *can* find a little sliver of meat to go with them."

Lark stared for a moment at the plate set before her, then resignedly picked up her fork.

"You'll have more meat tomorrow, Danny," Philippa said, "but I know *you* want more potatoes." He handed her the plate without a word. Philippa then put plenty of potatoes on her own plate.

Her form of etiquette usually required that she keep some sort of conversation going during a meal. Tonight, however, Philippa was obviously preoccupied, and all the potatoes were finished with hardly a word passed between them. While Philippa brooded, Lark and Danny cleared the table and brought on the next course. But by the time everyone had a large helping of salad and a piece of warm bread with butter and sharp cheese, Philippa had reached the point where she could no longer keep her thoughts to herself.

Just as she set her fork down to speak, Islington trotted in with something in his mouth. Philippa always left the front door open for him, so that he could come and go as he pleased. (She seemed to be impervious to cold, and naturally assumed that everyone else was the same.) The cat jumped onto Philippa's lap, then up onto the table, where he deposited a tiny, quivering brown creature.

"What have you got there, darling?" Philippa cooed. She watched the stunned vole stagger helplessly about beside her plate, then gingerly picked up the little animal by its tail. "An omen," she said, holding it out to Danny. "Please take this poor creature outside."

"If anybody happens to come by here in a week or so, *we* may be in the same state as that vole," Philippa was saying to Lark as Danny returned to his place.

"You mean you want to stay?" Danny said. "You've decided to stay?"

"I never *said* we were going to leave. Of course I want to stay. It's going to take an awful lot to get me to leave this house . . . I feel so at home here . . ."

"Oh, it's so much nicer than at my house," Lark said. "I wish I could stay here all the time."

"How sweet of you," Philippa said tonelessly.

"Even with some unknown person sneaking around and building fires?" Danny said.

"I'll get a new lock," said Philippa. "And mind you, I'm not guaranteeing a thing. It all depends on what else happens, and how successfully we can manage to deal with the situation. And by that I do *not* mean that you should go snooping and prying about. Oh, I'm not so dim-witted that I can't make a good guess at what you were whispering about before. I can tell that you two have the idea that you're these brilliant child detectives or something, and that this so-called 'mystery' seems like an adventure to you"—Danny started to interrupt, but she waved him down—"and that's just the kind of attitude that will get us in real trouble. If we keep people out of here, and let them see that we don't care what they do as long as it doesn't affect us, then perhaps they will learn to leave us alone.

But if you go getting involved in things that aren't your business, it will never work out."

"But what did we do wrong?" Danny said.

"Nothing, yet. It's your whole attitude that makes me so angry. And I *am* angry. I know you don't have the courage or the nerve to get into anything really dangerous, but I just hope you realize that it's exciting just to live in a place like this, you don't need to look for adventures. If things don't work out here, it won't be *my* fault. Eat your salad."

Lark and Danny washed the dishes; Philippa didn't want to put her burned hand in greasy water. They began to giggle as they worked. Philippa's remarks hadn't been particularly pleasant or humorous, but at least they indicated that she was no longer thinking of leaving; and Lark and Danny both felt rather light-headed with relief. Everything seemed funny: the gurgle of the faucet, the dainty flowers on the plates, the glass Lark almost dropped. "Whoops!" she whispered, and they giggled all the more. Danny knew that they should try to calm down; Philippa, nursing her hand in the living room, was still angry, even after her outburst; and their mirth, which excluded her, would make her feel even worse. But he could not help himself. When she called to them, her voice tense and bitter, to take the pie out of the oven (they were to eat it in the living room, by the fire), he made a face at her through the wall, and he and Lark couldn't keep from laughing. How funny it all was; how funny that she should be so serious. The room spun with their hysteria as Lark bent down and opened the oven door. Her hands were soapy, the pie was hot, and before she knew it, it was flattened upside down on the kitchen floor.

"Oh, no!" she gasped. It was too much. Clutching their sides, they rolled against the sink in helpless, hilarious agony.

Almost at once, Philippa was standing in the kitchen doorway. The instant they saw her face, their laughter died. "Oh," Lark stammered, "oh, I'm sorry. I'm so sorry."

Philippa's lips were shaking. "And just *what* is so bloody funny about ruining something I slaved over? What, may I ask?"

"We can eat it anyway," Danny said.

"We can*not* eat it anyway!" Her eyes glistened. "Oh, you . . . you monsters!" she shouted. "I can't bear the sight of you!" She turned from the kitchen, dashed loudly up the stairs, and slammed her bedroom door.

When the kitchen floor had been scrubbed and the dishes finished, Lark and Danny sat for a while in the large, dark living room. The firelight danced across the beamed ceiling and into their remorseful, downcast faces. Lark, they both knew, couldn't have made a worse impression.

Then Danny remembered about their visitor the night before, and, eager for a chance to make conversation, told her what had happened, and who Mr. Creech had thought the strange man was.

"Well," she said when he had finished, "he didn't actually *say* he'd seen Mary Peachy."

"But he said he thought it might be her. And her name was obviously carved there about three hundred years ago."

"Well, I don't actually know very much about Lord Harleigh, hardly anyone does, but he's supposed to be quite batty. The one thing I do know is something that happened to my father once, and even that isn't much."

"What happened?"

"Well, a few years ago, Lord Harleigh must have heard that my father was living here, and sent word that he wanted to commission my father to do some kind of painting for him. My father was quite pleased about it, since Lord Harleigh lives in the local manor house and must have a lot of money. He left whistling"—she paused, and her voice dropped,—"and came back only about an hour later, looking pale and shaken. He had a drink at once, and told me the commission was off."

"But why? Wouldn't he tell you?"

"He said he'd changed his mind, he'd rather do his own work, and we really didn't need the money. Which wasn't true, we *did* need the money quite badly then."

"But what made him change his mind? Don't you know?"

"All I know is that he looked . . . *frightened.* I'd never seen him look that way before. And he wouldn't talk about it."

Danny thought again of Lord Harleigh's voice, and felt his skin crawl. For a moment they sat and watched the fire without speaking. It was almost out now, and the room was so dark that he could hardly see Lark sitting close beside him. The wind rattled at the front door.

"Maybe we should go to bed," he said, standing up.

"Yes," Lark said, looking toward the dark part of the room, "I suppose that would be a good idea."

Very soon they were huddled in their beds under piles of blankets. The moment Danny closed his eyes he was asleep.

* * *

There were figures all around, vague and shadowy but with distinct livid faces. They were moaning softly, painfully. They were sprawling on the floor, crouching in corners, leaning against the walls. Danny stepped through them carefully, trying not to touch them, avoiding their eyes. The room seemed endless, but in the distance there was a window, a window filled with bright yellow light. He had to reach it. But the people kept getting in his way. His foot brushed against someone's head and the grinning, puffy face lolled over. A heavy body toppled against him and almost knocked him down. The window was getting closer, but the bodies around him were thicker and seemed to be pulling at him. He struggled against them, feeling the warm, moist touch of their flesh at every step. Outside the window he could see the view from the ridge, the Black Swan, and fields rolling clearly into the distance. It was spring, and everything was green. Just as he put his hand on the windowsill he heard a woman's laugh, and the window went black. He was lost. The laughter echoed all around him.

And as he struggled, moaning, to consciousness, the laughter was still there. The same laughter he had heard the other night. This time, too, it faded away quickly, but remained just long enough to leave him wondering again if it had been part of the dream, or if it had been real. He drew his head under the blankets and pressed his body against the wall. He was afraid, but not terrified as he had been the last time. Half asleep, he was able to keep from thinking about what the laughter could mean. He only knew that it was pleasant laughter, gay, mischievous. He somehow felt that he would like the girl who laughed that way.

When he closed his eyes the dream ran clearly through his mind. He had been in the living room downstairs, but the room had been much longer, and he remembered the feeling of not getting anywhere as he walked and walked. Just before he fell into a deep, dreamless sleep he realized that in the dream the cellar door had been new, the hinges shiny. And there were no names on the door at all.

13

Then, for a while, things seemed to quiet down. Of course there were all the little, unexpected events that naturally occur when city dwellers move to a primitive, secluded house. Lil got stuck in the mud during a heavy rain and Philippa and Danny had to subsist on potatoes and canned molasses for three days. (Philippa didn't mind as much as she pretended.) The two of them made the awful discovery that it was an absolute necessity to empty the large metal can in the outhouse every week or so. This involved digging a deep hole in some out-of-the-way corner of the yard, then lugging the heavy can, its contents slopping over at the edges, all the way from the outhouse to the hole, then averting one's face and dumping it all into the hole, then filling up the hole, then washing out the can with water from the rainwater tank, then returning it to the outhouse again. Philippa tried to make the tiny room a little more pleasant by filling it with fragrant pine branches, and she pasted up some magazine pictures of youths on Greek vases.

At first, bathing too made them both secretly yearn for London plumbing, but as time went on they actually began to enjoy the ritual of it. There was a large white enamel hip bath in Philippa's bedroom. To use it, all their little pots had to be filled with water and heated in the kitchen. Then, one by one (they hadn't yet bought a pail), each pot was carried up the winding stairs and dumped into the tub, filling the room with clouds of steam. It was worth it all, though, to rip off one's clothes in the frigid atmosphere, then plunge into the heavenly, scalding water. Philippa learned to have her largest pot always full of water on the stove, so that in the morning, and at any other time when the icy well water was too much to bear, a bit of hot water would be ready.

Daily rituals were something they had to get used to. Danny was awakened every morning by the sound of Philippa pouring hot water into the small washbasin in his room. Then there was the awful moment of jumping out of his warm bed into the freezing morning air. The room was much colder than his bedroom in London had been, but somehow, perhaps because he knew that whatever comfort they would have during the day depended on the tasks that only he could perform, he had little trouble getting out of bed. He would rapidly pull on long woolen underwear, splash the steaming water on his hands and face, then hurry down to the cellar landing and immediately begin to pump. At first he hated this, but soon he discovered it was the best way to wake himself up, and even began to enjoy trying to do at least one more stroke every day. By breakfast time he was ravenous. In London it had been a struggle to face his single egg, but here he always ate at least three of the delicious country ones, and mounds of thick, charred toast.

Then, out under the gray sky, still palely streaked with early-morning color, he would wander among the heaving, sighing trees, his face stinging with the cold, and pick up pieces of dead wood scattered over the ground. Occasionally he would come upon a whole dead tree, and feeling very woodsmanlike (he only attempted the thinnest ones), he would either pull it down, or hack at it with the little ax. He loved watching them crash noisily to the ground through the other tree branches, but it was even more satisfying to stagger back to the house, to Philippa's cries of praise, with the trunk on his shoulder and the whole length of it dragging along behind him.

By the light of the Aladdin lamp, he would study at the round wooden table in front of the fire. He had done reasonably well at school in London, but it was due more to the way he could figure out just what the teacher wanted than to actual hard work. He had always been drowsy and inattentive in class, frequently even falling asleep in geometry, his closed eyes hidden by his hand. But here, whether from the invigorating cold air, or the strenuous exercise (something almost completely unknown to him before), his mind was unusually alert. History seemed much more real to him, because now he could more clearly imagine what it must have been like to be alive in other times.

Latin, and even math, were easier to concentrate on. And not only did he feel more alert, but for the first time in his life his mind was more concerned with what was actually going on, less apt to drift off into some vague dreamworld.

Lunch was usually eaten standing up in the kitchen, and consisted of a thick and crumbly ham or cheese sandwich and a mug of hot, milky tea. Afterward Danny would deal with any outdoor chores that were left. Frequently there were big pieces of wood to saw up into logs. On some days, after a heavy wind, he would have to gather up brush and twigs scattered over the yard, breaking them up to use for kindling, and prop up the lopsided arbor by the door. This was the time to carry coal up from the rapidly diminishing pile in the cellar, and to fill the lamps and the little kitchen burner with smelly oil. He always did this on the outside table which Lark had first used, but now he covered it carefully with newspaper to keep the spilled oil from seeping into the wood, for both he and Philippa were looking forward to the time when they would be able to eat outside.

Islington had his job too, and he enjoyed it thoroughly. Much of the time he was nowhere to be seen, but then he would suddenly appear, dashing madly past the house or inside it at the heels of a frantic, squealing little mouse or vole. He enjoyed playing games with the poor creatures, and would chase one into a corner and then just sit there, staring at the quivering ball of fur, or bat it violently about with his paws. Sometimes he would eat it, but most often he just trotted upstairs with the body in his mouth and dropped it on Philippa's bed as a gift, and to show her how useful he was being. It was a rare day that she didn't find one or more of them sprawled out on her pillow when she opened her eyes in the morning.

When his afternoon chores were over, and his studying for the most part was out of the way, Danny liked to wander across the hill. The tumuli, with their odd aura of magnificent bleakness and elemental, almost supernatural power, drew him frequently; and he would spend many hours there with no idea of how much time was going by. He loved it there on the rare sunny days, when he could see the ocean, and cloud shadows would fly, undulating, over the hills and valleys spread below. He loved it too when it was dark and threatening, when distant trees would toss and sway and the wind keened all around him.

Once, when a storm was approaching, he couldn't bear to leave, but stood up on one of the mounds and watched as the black clouds and silvery rain swept toward him from the sea. The thunder seemed more passionate here, like the expression of some gargantuan rage, and the rain was a million speeding fingers, brittle and cold, drenching him instantly. Lightning reached out at the villages like palsied hands, but Danny did not move, feeling somehow protected by the mystical power of the tumuli. And the storm passed over him quickly, leaving him strangely breathless, his heart pounding and his spirits surging inside him. Philippa was almost wild when he got home, his clothes plastered to his shivering body. She was as wet as he, for she had been running out into the yard to call him, then dashing back inside at every loud clap of thunder.

Another time, coming back from the tumuli just at nightfall, he noticed a figure standing at the edge of the wood as he emerged from the thicket of pines. He stopped. The person had not heard him, and continued standing there, just watching the house. He was less than four feet tall, and at first Danny thought he was a child. But then he noticed how short his arms and legs were, how large his torso and his head, and how sad and wrinkled his face was in the cold evening light. Danny moved to get a closer look, and the dwarf spun around to face him, his eyes glinting like a cat's. He looked at Danny for an instant, an odd smile on his heavy face, and then waddled quickly away into the woods behind him. Danny hurried into the house. He did not mention the incident to Philippa.

For the first week or so, Danny wondered about Mr. Bexford, who was still his legal guardian. He had never bothered much with Danny, but that did not mean that he would simply forget about him now. As long as the lawyer knew that Danny was leading a safe and orderly life, as he had done in London, there really wasn't any reason for him to do anything more than send Danny his check once a year. But it was quite a different thing for a ward simply to disappear, and Danny was sure that inevitably Mr. Bexford would learn of it. Though busy and preoccupied, the lawyer was nevertheless very scrupulous and correct, and would probably go to great lengths to find his vanished charge. Would he alert the police? Danny wondered. Would he run a photo in the papers? And once Mr. Bexford did find him, would he take him away from here? Then what would happen to him? Had he committed a crime? Would he be sent to some horrible reform school?

These worries gave a rather insecure quality to Danny's first days at Blackbriar, but as time went on he began to think about them less and less. The world of London and his old life began to seem far away and unreal, and soon took up very little of his thoughts.

But as this worry faded, another took its place. After those first two days, he had seen Lark very rarely. He had hoped to be seeing her all the time. He wondered if it would have been any different if Philippa had never met or heard about her. True, Lark had to go to school, which was inconvenient (the holidays had ended), and it would have been difficult for him to see her secretly very often; but still, it was usually Philippa who got in the way of their meeting. She would frequently find some chore he had to do, some errand or trip they had to go on that did not include Lark. And Philippa was very cautious about inviting the girl to Blackbriar. "It isn't fair to subject her to the danger we are in," she would say. "Her father would *never* forgive me if anything should happen." But when Danny would retort with, "If you really thought we were in danger, you wouldn't want to stay here, either," Philippa would have no answer. Sometimes Danny did visit her when he was supposed to be in the library, and occasionally Philippa would relent and invite her up to the house; but Danny certainly didn't see her as much as he would have liked.

Of course, he understood what Philippa was trying to do; but this time it was different from the way it had been with Tony Bramble and the others in London—for this time Danny was determined. Over and over again he insisted to himself that he must not let her stop his friendship with Lark. And he could see that Philippa suspected this change. She was always watching him. Frequently he would look up to find her eyes on his face, as though she were trying, by looking closely enough, to see what was going on inside his head.

But she never actually forbade him to see Lark, or really spoke against her, as she had done with the others in London. Danny's new determination seemed to be forcing her to tread more cautiously; and his knowledge that it was having an effect made his determination all the stronger.

At night, Danny continued to dream.

Not every night, but frequently, dreams more vivid than any he had had in London would wake him in the darkness. Sometimes he would dream of the tumuli, of the strange procession there. But most frequently he dreamed what he began to call his pesthouse dream, in which he tried to push his way through the pale, groping figures in the living room, never quite reaching the open window. No dream was ever repeated exactly, but in one way all were the same: he always awoke to half-heard laughter; laughter so distant, so quickly fading, that he never failed to wonder if it had really been there.

14

A couple of times a week they drove to town in the afternoon. Philippa shopped for food and supplies, and Danny either explored the twisting cobblestone streets or spent his time in the library, returning books, getting out new ones, and doing research. The old librarian who had once questioned Danny so intensely was not always there; and when he was, he behaved as though Danny were a stranger to him, casting down his eyes and stamping the cards without a word.

Late one afternoon, having grown tired of his Latin translation, Danny found himself wandering aimlessly through the stacks. The dim, labyrinthine passages, lined with faded volumes, seemed mysterious and intriguing to him; and on this day he moved quietly through them, running his hand vaguely along the dusty spines, hardly pausing to read the titles. He had climbed several of the narrow iron staircases, and now rather enjoyed not knowing quite where he was, or how to get back to the reading room. The stacks were kept unlit; anyone wanting to see more clearly could switch on a light at the end of each row, but today Danny preferred to walk in the dark, relishing the slightly uneasy sensation of not being able to see where the passage led, or what was in the next aisle.

Suddenly he stopped. There were voices coming from somewhere quite near him. He felt a shiver of excitement. How perfect it was, to be exploring this eerie place (which of course was really perfectly safe, he told himself), and then to hear a conversation he could secretly listen to. Cautiously he crept toward the voices. The aisle ended at a narrow corridor. In the wall across from him was a door, a little to his left, directly opposite the aisle which ran next to his. The door was slightly open, emitting a thin crack of light. The voices were coming from behind it. He took one step backwards, into deeper shadow, then leaned forward, straining his ears.

"—can't understand why it seems to bother you so little. It's a bit more than just inconvenient, after all."

Danny recognized the librarian's voice at once. The one time he had spoken to him, Danny remembered with mounting excitement, the man had obviously known something about Blackbriar which he didn't want to tell. Perhaps there was a chance that he might even say something about it now.

"You have always been an alarmist," said the other voice. It was a voice with a slight lisp to it, and Danny felt a sudden icy pang in his stomach. The feeling that the

stacks were basically a place of safety quickly drained,
away. The other person in the room was Lord Harleigh.

Perhaps it *is* rather unscrupulous of me to eavesdrop on
them, Danny thought for an instant; but then he discarded
the thought with disgust, as simply an attempt to rational-
ize his fear.

"Too much of an alarmist, I think," Lord Harleigh went
on. Although his voice was slow, there was a note of
annoyance in it. "If we'd bought the house, as I wanted, we
wouldn't be having this little difficulty. But no, *you* were
against buying it, and now look what has happened."

"I'm sorry," said the librarian. He cleared his throat
nervously. "It *is* my fault. But please, don't hold it against
me. I—I thought it was best. I was afraid that if you bought
it, you would draw attention to us, that people might begin
to suspect the connection we have to the place."

Lord Harleigh laughed dryly. "As if they didn't already.
Why do you think it was for sale for such a long time? No
one around here dares to go near it. It's only because these
people are from far away that they are foolhardy enough to
buy the place, let alone remain there for so long."

There was no longer any doubt in Danny's mind as to
what place they were talking about, or which people they
meant. But why "foolhardy," he wondered. That must mean
there really was danger there. . . .

"Well," said the librarian, "perhaps I am an alarmist.
But there is something you don't know, something I've
learned from Ivor since you and I met last week. Do you
remember that artist, Hovington, the one whom you actually invited to your house when—"

"Yes, yes, I know the man," said Lord Harleigh irritably.

"I can certainly see that you must have had your—ahem—*motives* for asking him, but it was an unfortunate occurrence nonetheless," the librarian wheezed, and cleared his throat. "You are aware, I think, that he has a daughter, a child, with whom he lives alone. And who knows what he might have told her about that little visit—"

"He has told her nothing," Lord Harleigh snapped. "He wouldn't dare."

"Nevertheless, the possibility exists. Which in itself would not be alarming, except for the fact that she has been seen with them, at Blackbriar." He paused, as if to give the statement more impact. "Somehow," he went on, "she must have become friends with the boy. Now, we don't know what she knows, we don't know what *they* know, but together they might have discovered something, and—"

"What of it? Many people know *something*. It is no threat to us."

"But there is a difference here. Not only are they all from the city, and therefore immune to the fears and prejudices which rule the people in this area; but there they are, ensconced in our most vulnerable spot, what we might call our very underbelly, pale and soft and unprotected . . ."

Danny's foot had gone to sleep. Silently, he tried to move it without losing his balance.

"But there is something you fail to see." Lord Harleigh had stopped whispering. He seemed angry, and involuntarily Danny stepped back. "*We* are not the vulnerable ones. *They* are. They may have some vague suspicions, but they certainly couldn't be aware of—"

On the word "vulnerable" Danny had reached out his hand to steady himself. Vulnerable? he thought. Vulnerable to—? His hand, with his weight behind it, came to rest against a book. Quickly he drew it back, but too late. With a noise that seemed to him like thunder, three books in the next aisle tumbled to the floor.

"What was that?" Lord Harleigh hissed. The door swung open and the librarian peered anxiously out into the hallway. Danny shrank back into deeper shadow. The librarian craned his head forward, his jowls swinging slowly as he moved his head from side to side. For an instant he seemed to be staring right at Danny; then his head turned away. "Mice," he said, "this place is infested with them." But as he stepped back into the room he closed the door firmly.

Danny's heart was making such a noise that he could barely hear anything else; and now that the door was closed whispers were almost completely indistinct. Leave! he shouted to himself, leave before they do, while it's safe, while the door is closed!

But something, something new inside him, would not allow him to leave while there was still a chance of hearing more. Almost against his will he moved closer, straining his ears.

But all he could hear were scattered words and phrases.

". . . underneath . . . coming all too soon . . . terrify . . . rid of them . . . that cat . . . magnificent creature . . ."

Danny moved closer.

". . . what we could do with the beast . . ."

Do with him? What could they want to do with him? And was Lord Harleigh giggling?

". . . marvelous opportunity for . . . really horrify them . . . what we have been doing . . . anyone would be . . ."

He sighed in frustration. How could he have been so clumsy? And just when he was about to learn something definite! It really doesn't make sense to stay any longer, he told himself, and at that moment he heard a chair scraping behind the door. Instantly he moved backwards and crouched down near the floor.

Someone tall and lean stepped out of the room, followed by the shorter figure of the librarian. Danny could only partially see them through the space above a row of books on the shelf that separated his aisle from the one in which they stood. He had never really seen Lord Harleigh's face clearly, and now he half hoped, half dreaded that it would come into view.

"That noise we heard," Lord Harleigh said. "It might very well have been a mouse, but I think that perhaps we should find another place for our weekly conferences. But let us discuss it at another time. Good day." He moved away down the aisle without turning in Danny's direction.

As Lord Harleigh's footsteps faded down the iron stairway, the librarian moved to the place where the books had fallen. They had left a gap directly across from where Danny was crouching. The librarian squatted down and picked them up; then, his face on a level with Danny's, looked through the hole.

Danny held his breath, inhaling a large quantity of dust. His nose and throat tickled unbearably. How could he possibly not see me? he thought wildly. But, not seeming to notice him, the librarian put one book in place, then the second. The third, however, seemed to interest him, and still squatting he carefully opened it and resolutely began turning one page after another. Danny knew that if he dared to breathe he would cough; but his chest was beginning to ache, and the impulse to take a breath was almost too strong to fight. Get away! Get away! he screamed silently at the man.

And finally, as if in answer to Danny's thought, the librarian slowly put the book in place, stood up, brushed off his knees, and returned to his office, closing the door.

Danny breathed, and a muffled cough broke out of him. He waited tensely, but there was no response from the librarian's office.

Then, for several minutes, as his heart slowed down and he began to notice the clammy feeling of sweat over his body, he simply stayed where he was. The words of the conversation repeated themselves over and over again in his head, ominous and confusing. He had learned very little of a definite nature that he hadn't already known; only that he, Philippa, and Lark really were in some kind of danger. He had no idea what to do about it, but realized now that what was happening to them was not a game. It was something very real, and perhaps very threatening.

When it seemed as though he had waited long enough for Lord Harleigh to be well out of the library, he stood up shakily and began making his way toward the reading room.

15

"And on top of it all, I just can't decide whether or not to tell Philippa, or how much to tell her, or what," Danny was saying. It was the next afternoon, and he and Lark were on their way up to Blackbriar on foot. (Philippa was at the hairdresser. "I can't go on like this for another instant," she had said. "I've got to do something about all this confusion up here. I always think better when my hair is in order." The thought of the appointment put her in such a good mood that she had dropped Danny off at the Black Swan on her way, with permission, reluctant though it was, to bring Lark back up for dinner and the night.)

"I mean," he went on, "of course it seems like she ought to know, it all sounds so threatening, and she is just as involved as anyone. But I'm so afraid she'll just decide to pack up and leave; this is exactly the kind of thing she was afraid of."

They passed through the first gate and started across the field. The sunset was spread across the sky, coldly gilding the surrounding hilltops. Mournful evening birdcalls broke the sound of the wind. For a while neither of them spoke as they tramped across the wet grass toward the black-green shape of the woods beyond the distant gate.

"God, I don't know *what* to say," Lark said softly. Danny watched the clouds of her breath fade quickly away with every word.

"Maybe we should ask your father. He might know what to do."

"I don't know. I'm sort of afraid to. I could tell he was *determined* not to have anything to do with Lord Harleigh again."

"But it's not your fault. It isn't anybody's fault. We just kind of fell into this."

"I know. But he won't see it that way."

As the forest loomed closer the light began to fade more quickly, and just a few steps in among the trees it was almost as dark as night. They had to keep their eyes fastened on the track to avoid sliding into deep, muddy ruts. The birdcalls were louder here, more threatening, and the underbrush rustled with the movement of unseen things.

"I've never walked through here at night," Lark said.

"Neither have I."

"And it always seems to take so long when we're driving . . ."

"Maybe the moon will come out, then well be able to see better."

They trudged on. Occasionally one of them would slip and grab the other for support. Eventually the moon did appear, moving jerkily through the tree branches as they walked, rippling in the puddles beneath their feet. It was easier to see, but they kept their eyes straight ahead, never looking into the forest on either side.

"What if there's another fire burning when we get back?" Danny said suddenly.

Lark stopped and grabbed his arm. "*Why* do you have to say that?"

"Oh, there *won't* be. I was only kidding. Come on, let's keep going or we'll never get there." He gave her arm a gentle tug and they moved on.

At last they turned the final bend in the track. There was the house straight ahead, clearly visible, for the moon was hanging just above the chimney, filling the clearing with light. And the light flickering from the living room window, the firelight, fell toward them across the clearing in a bright yellow patch.

"Oh, no," Lark said, clinging to Danny's arm as she stepped backwards, "oh, no."

"Oh, yes," Danny said.

They hung together just inside the trees, until Danny took a deep breath and said, "I'm going to look inside. We haven't been gone that long, they won't expect us back, especially without the car. We've got to find out how they get inside. Philippa put another lock on the door the other time this happened, so they couldn't be using an old key. We won't have this chance again, surprising them without the car."

"How *can* you? I can't bear the thought of going any closer. I won't let you, I'll scream if you do!"

Though his whole body felt tightened with fear, Danny almost smiled. How brave and tough she had tried to seem the first time he had met her, how foolish and weak she had made him feel! Now his fear was like nervous energy, pushing him forward instead of holding him back; and he felt a strange kind of pleasure in insisting that they do what *he* wanted. "But we've got to at least look inside!" he said. "Don't you see? They won't be expecting us."

Slowly they moved across the yard. It seemed to take forever. Danny reached the window, Lark crouched behind him. He moved his head just a fraction of an inch, so that one eye only was peering inside. And this time there was someone there, a figure crouching at the hearth, rapidly feeding log after log into the already considerable blaze. His lean, athletic body was clothed in tight-fitting black, but Danny couldn't see who he was, for though the man continually turned his head from side to side, as if making sure he was not being watched, he didn't turn it far enough so that the firelight made his features clear. Very soon he stood up, brushed off his hands, and picked up the lantern beside him. Then, as the man checked the room once again, Danny caught a brief glimpse of a thin face with large, soft lips, framed by a mass of curling, shoulder-length hair.

As soon as he had looked once around the room, the young man pulled open the cellar door, stepped inside, and slammed it behind him. Danny saw the light from his lantern grow dimmer behind the large space at the bottom of the door until it disappeared altogether.

"Come on," he whispered, "we're going in now."

"Going in?" She sounded incredulous. "But who's there?"

"A young chap. He's down in the cellar now. And I'll bet he's just as scared as we are. If we're quiet, he won't hear us going in, and maybe we can surprise him down there. He has no weapon, and . . . he doesn't look like the kind of person who would hurt us."

"But why do we have to go in at all?"

"Why, to find out who he is, of course, and where he's from and why he did this."

There were two locks on the door now. Danny opened them without a sound. The large flashlight was just inside, but he did not turn it on as they crept past the fireplace to the cellar door. They paused. For a second, he wondered if he would be doing this if he hadn't noticed how gentle and unsure of himself the young intruder's face and movements had seemed.

And then he switched on the light, pulled open the door, and dashed down the steps. He swung the beam around the room again and again, not stopping until he felt Lark touch his shoulder.

The cellar was empty.

For a moment Danny wondered if he might be going mad. "But I saw him go down here, I know I did," he said.

"Are you sure?"

"Of course. I know what I see." He stepped down onto the stone floor and swung his flashlight around once again. There was certainly no one in the room.

"Wait a minute," Lark said. "Turn off the flashlight."

"Why?"

"Just turn it off. I think I see something."

"But—"

She reached over and flipped the switch. There were no windows in the cellar and for a moment they could see nothing.

"What good is this going to do?" Danny said pettishly.

"Please, just wait a minute. I think I might have seen something, and this is the only way to find out."

As their eyes adjusted to the darkness they could see that only a trickle of pale moonlight was coming in through the coal chute. But, oddly, there was enough light in the room to see everything, dimly but clearly.

"You don't think he could have gotten out through the coal chute?" Danny said. "He didn't have time, and it's too small anyway."

"No, he didn't. But look over there," and she pointed to the opposite corner of the room, where a rusty bedspring leaned against the wall. "I *knew* I saw something there."

Yellow light was coming from the corner, filtering through the bedspring from somewhere behind, pausing to rest on an occasional mangled metal curlicue. "But where's it *coming* from?" Danny cried, and ran over. The spring seemed almost like a cage, blocking one corner, and Danny was not surprised that he had never noticed anything here before. But in a moment Lark was down on her hands and knees, and found that with not too much trouble she could squeeze her way behind it.

"Quick!" she cried, "Danny! Come in here!" And scraping his hands on the floor, he crawled in behind her.

There, its bottom about a foot from the floor, was a tiny wooden door, only four feet high and three feet wide. Light was coming in through the cracked, rotting boards, and the door hung slightly open, so that even more light came through the edge.

"It's so crowded back here, how do we get it open?" Danny grunted, pushing himself back against the bed-spring as Lark tried to slide over to make enough room to open the door a bit more. When they had squeezed together into a space that seemed much too small for two people, Lark gave the door a strong push and it swung slowly open, creaking gently.

Danny gasped and Lark almost cried out. They had not known what to expect; what they saw was a stone passage-way. Tunnel-like at first, it quickly became high enough for a man to stand upright. The arching ceiling was also of stone, supported by thick wooden beams.

Rubbing uncomfortably against each other, Lark and Danny slid over so that they could see deeper inside. At first it seemed as though the passage ended after about ten feet, but they quickly realized, from the way the ceiling sloped and turned at the end, that it must lead to a descending flight of steps. The light was coming from a torch stuck into a bracket in the wall at the point where the stairway began.

"My God," Lark whispered.

"He must have forgotten to blow out the torch," Danny said. He reached over and touched a hook on the inside of the door. "*And* to lock the door."

"He must have been in a real hurry."

"I told you he looked scared. It's lucky for us that he was."

All at once Danny noticed how uncomfortable they were. "Well, we can't just stay here, all squeezed up like this," he said.

"You don't expect us to go *down* there, do you?"

"Well, we've got to go down it sometime, and now might be the best time. That man was just here, so it'll probably be a while before somebody uses it again. And the door's unlocked. They might not be so forgetful next time."

Lark shivered. "I suppose this means there's got to be a next time. How awful to think that people, from somewhere, are going to be coming in and out of the house, while you're away, while you're asleep in your beds . . ."

"Don't keep saying 'you.' You're here too, you know, it's too late for you to get out of it now."

"But do you really mean to keep living here? I suppose it's obvious that this fellow was sent by Lord Harleigh, and after what you heard yesterday there's no question but that they want to harm us. You're just not safe anymore. I think we should tell the police."

"But I don't really think they will harm us." He tried to shift into a more comfortable position. "They seem to be afraid of any attention, and they'd get attention if anyone was hurt. I mean, I bet they'd rather have us here than a lot of policemen poking around. And we can't tell the police because what do we have to tell them? That I overheard a conversation? I think all Lord Harleigh wants to do is scare us. That's what they've been trying to do."

"So what do you propose to do, then?"

"Explore this passageway, of course."

"Now?"

"Now."

Lark sighed angrily. "But we *can't* go now. Philippa will be back any minute, and I'm sure you don't want her to know about this."

"But now's the only safe time to go, since they've just used it. We'll just leave Philippa a note saying we went for a walk. This tunnel couldn't go on that long, it must lead to someplace quite near here. When we come out we can just walk back to the house as if nothing had happened."

In a few moments they were ready to go. Fastened to the front door was a hastily scrawled note saying, "Dear P., We went for a walk, be back soon. Love L. and D." Lark brought the smaller flashlight. Leaving the door unlocked, as they had found it, they crawled into the narrow passageway. When they reached the place where it grew wider they stood up, brushing off their knees, and stepped over to the stairway.

The stone steps were steep and very narrow, and wound in such a tight spiral that they could not see beyond the sixth step. Slowly they started down, constantly switching their beams of light from the steps of the walls around them. Very soon the stairway had made a complete turn, and they could no longer see the light from the torch behind them.

"Hey," Danny said, "it keeps going. I thought it was only going to be a few steps."

"So did I."

As they went on the air began to grow colder and damper. Their breath was as thick as kitchen steam. Water dripped all around them, making eerie metallic noises as it struck the stone.

They reached a landing. Only a small one, for they could see where the steps began again after a few feet. To the left was a stone archway with a room behind it. Danny sent his light through the doorway and it hit a bare stone wall about ten feet away.

"Just a small room," he said, and stepped in. Lark, just behind him, almost tripped over something on the floor, and cursing, pointed her flashlight at her feet.

Her shriek echoed all around them.

"My God!" Danny cried, spinning around, "What—?"

With her cry still ringing, distorted, through distant stone passageways, Danny saw Lark stagger back against the wall. At her feet a human skull rolled crazily for a moment, then came to a rest, its vacant eyes gaping at him from the threshold.

"Oh, no," he whispered. Shivering, he felt sweat break out over his whole body. And from the center of the floor he played his shaking light over the whole room.

The floor was covered with bones. Most of them lay rather neatly around the walls. The heads, rib cages, pelvises, legs and arms were all in their proper relation to one another, so that it was obvious that many bodies had been carefully laid out here. Over the years the flesh had rotted away, leaving only the clean white bones.

Danny shook Lark's shoulder very gently. Her eyes were closed. "Hey, come on," he said, trying to keep his voice from shaking. "Open up, it's not so bad. They're all dead, they're not going to hurt you."

"No," she whispered. "I don't want to see. I want to get out of here, I want to go home, but I can't move."

"Please, don't be like that." He turned and quickly examined the bones once more, his hand still on her shoulder. "Don't you know what this is? It's terribly exciting." Her eyes remained tightly shut. "This . . . is one of the answers. This must be what Mary Peachy did with all the bodies."

Her eyes blinked open, but she kept them focused on his face. "How do you know that? How do you know they're not just . . . the other people who wandered down here?"

"How could they be? They're all in the same condition, they must have all been put here around the same time. And it must have been a long time ago, it takes a while for everything to rot away so completely."

She glanced at her feet, then for a second at the other side of the room. She shook her head quickly, then said, "I'm sorry. I was just so shocked and surprised."

She stepped away from the wall. Danny still had his hand on her shoulder. They were standing very close together. For the first time Danny felt truly stronger than she, responsible and protective. Somehow it was a beautiful feeling, filling his body with an unknown, intense kind of warmth. "I—" he started to say. They were looking into each other's eyes. Suddenly she leaned forward, and they kissed.

Quickly Danny stepped away. "Oh," he said. "Well, are you all right now?" He felt himself blush.

She was smiling, and, helplessly, so was he. "Yes," she

said, "I'm fine." She held up her light, and once more they looked around the room. And why was it that the bones were no longer menacing, only lonely and sad?

"I guess you must be right about them," she said. "It all fits together. If only there was some way we could know for sure that these were the people on the door."

Danny examined some of the bones more closely. Lark, still trembling slightly, remained on the threshold. "They've got to be," Danny said finally, coming back to her. "Their names on the cellar door make it just like a gravestone, and here, beyond the door, are all these people. They've got to be the same ones."

"I suppose the only way we'll really ever know is if we find Mary Peachy."

"I wonder if one of these is her," Danny said. "I guess, when she knew she was going to die, she could have just crawled down here with the others."

"But then she would have put *her* date on the door too."

"I know. And somehow I think her fate was different from everyone else's. I don't know why." He glanced back into the room once more, then they both walked across the landing to the next flight of stairs.

These stairs, though made of stone, were obviously newer than the others, much more squarely, neatly made. And they did not turn, but plunged down in a straight line so very far that they could not see to the end.

"God, it makes me dizzy," Lark said, taking a step back.

"This is incredible! Where could it possibly go? These are so much newer than the rest. Who would go to all the trouble to build something like this? It's insane!"

"Think," Lark said, "it certainly is insane . . ."

"Lord Harleigh! Of course. Why, these steps must go all the way down, the hill, to Harleigh Manor. *That's* what the librarian meant about the 'soft underbelly' or whatever."

"And that's where the fellow who built the fire came from."

"Well . . . I suppose we really can't go down there now," said Danny quickly. "It would take us forever, and Philippa would go mad with worry."

"We've done enough today," Lark said, sounding relieved. "Let's save *something* for another time."

Philippa had not yet returned when they got back up to the house. So much had happened that the time had seemed longer than it actually was. The first thing they did was to move the bedspring right up against the tunnel door, so that anyone trying to come into the house that way would be unable to get through unless he could manage to knock over the spring by pushing open the door. This feat, if possible, would require great strength as well as produce a tremendous noise. "Now," Lark said, "we'll know for sure if anybody gets in."

"Plus," Danny added, "it won't give it away that we know about the tunnel. I mean, we could have just moved the spring against the wall to get it out of the way."

The old door that led down to the cellar had no lock, but the latch was on the living room side. After closing the latch, they took down the note from the front door, lit the lamps, built up the fire, and when Philippa finally did arrive, her hair an unreal, shining orb, they had just about got the coal stove going. They did not mention the tunnel.

Danny did not sleep well that night. And when he awoke in the darkness, with the familiar laughter fading away above the pounding of his heart, he felt the old, nightmare fear more strongly than ever.

Then he noticed that there was a light coming from Lark's room. He got out of bed. Now she'll know what I mean, he told himself, now she's heard it too. What a relief to know at last where it's coming from. As he stepped into Lark's room he heard the reassuring sound of Philippa's snores coming from the room beyond.

Lark was sitting up tensely in her bed, a candle burning at the table by her side. "Oh, hullo," she said quickly. "I can't stop thinking about the tunnel, and I can't sleep either because I keep thinking I hear somebody pushing over the spring."

"What about that laughter! Now do you see what it's like?"

"What laughter?"

"Didn't you just hear it?"

"Oh, you mean that dream you have. No, why should I have heard it?"

"But it's not a dream, I always hear it after I wake up. You've been awake, you're not even reading, you *must* have heard it!"

"I didn't hear a thing. Don't get so emotional. It's only a dream."

"But I tell you, I'm awake when I hear it, I could see the light from your room while it was going on." He slumped into the chair by the bed table. "After it died away I felt so relieved, knowing that it's just some girl down there, laughing in that passageway to frighten us. But if you didn't hear it, I still don't know what it is."

"Well, I didn't, and I've been listening to all sorts of real noises, so I know I would have heard it if it was there. It's just your imagination, and I'm not surprised, after what we saw today."

"But it sounds so real," he moaned. Suddenly he was strangely upset, clenching his hands together and rocking back and forth in the chair. "It sounds so very real."

16

Danny was awakened by a harsh scraping sound, then a blast of icy morning air. The steam from the hot water Philippa was pouring into his basin swirled in the gusts of raw wind blowing through the room.

Pulling the blankets tightly about him, he struggled to a sitting position. "Uh," he said hoarsely. "What happened? Did you open the *window*?"

"Of course I did!" She was beaming, red-cheeked, vibrantly alert. "Feel that air! Feel it! It's new today. You should be outside, not lounging around in this stuffy room." She planted her feet wide apart and took a deep breath, standing inches taller.

"That's all very nice, I'm sure," Danny said. "But I think I'll stay in bed a bit longer. I didn't get much sleep last night." He drew his head under the blankets.

But Philippa was in one of her whimsical moods and

wasn't going to give up easily. She raced to the bed and with one brisk motion ripped all the bedclothes right off. With the sheets and blankets dangling around her, she cried, "Spring is coming!"

"Super," Danny sighed, "just super."

But it was impossible to lie there uncovered. Mumbling, he got to his feet, turned to face the powerful blast, and looked out the window.

And it was true, something was different. Nothing obvious like buds on the trees, new grass, or even a cloudless blue sky. But there was a new freshness in the air, a faint suggestion of warmth in the sunlight that was coming down with unusual vigor, and a new clarity in the view down the tree-studded slope. Suddenly he felt like going outside.

"Maybe I'll go get some firewood," he said.

"Well," Philippa said, "at *last*. And you don't need to pump first, for a change," she added from the stairs. "I've got enough water for the time being."

He looked into Lark's room as soon as he was dressed. She still seemed to be asleep, and he decided that she was probably tired enough to be left in bed for a while longer. He sped down the stairs and, without a word to Philippa in the kitchen, out of the door.

And he was running, and the air was splashing around him, not warm, but stinging less than usual. The sky seemed distant, endless, as though the heavy, solid ceiling that had always been there had blown away. Everything was sparkling, shimmering, in some unknown way, even the mist that drifted among the trees. He leapt into the woods, reaching at branches, and for a time forgot that there was such a thing as firewood at all.

Later, out of breath, picking up sticks and branches, he tried to decide what was so different about the world today. It was hardly warmer, and there had been sunny days before. What was it? Only that the air, and the brown earth, and the barren trees, somehow seemed alive. And it was odd that such a subtle difference, something he could barely see or explain, could fill him with such boundless exuberance, an exuberance that was strangely close to tears.

Lark was wandering in the yard when he got back. "*Thanks* for waking me up," she said. "Thanks for telling me what it was like today. I've almost missed the best part!"

He dropped his bundle and spread his arms, and the emotion inside him burst out in thick, irrepressible laughter. And then, Lark was laughing too.

"Oh, I can't *bear* to go home today," she finally managed to say. "It's too lovely up here."

"Don't go home. We can do all sorts of things."

"But I have to go to school."

"Tomorrow you can say you were sick."

"But my father . . ."

"He'll think you went straight to school! If you stayed, we could go to the tumuli."

"Well, I hope Philippa won't object."

"She might not. This weather's made her mad."

Philippa was bustling about the morning chores with more than her usual gusto. She was practically twittering as she dashed around in the kitchen, darting outside every other minute to take a deep breath of air. "I'm *never* smoking another cigarette as long as I live!" she would cry, then rush back into the house to see if the toast was burning.

"Well," she said to them breathlessly in the yard, "do you think we should attempt it?"

"Attempt what?"

"Why, having breakfast outside, of course."

"Today?"

"Can you bear the thought of eating in that dreary hole of a dining room? *I* can't."

"But, Philippa," Danny explained, "I mean, I know it's a beautiful day and everything, but we'd freeze. We'd have to eat with our gloves on. The only way to keep warm out here is to keep moving. You've been running in and out of the house, you don't really know how cold it is."

"Yes," Lark said, "we wouldn't be at all comfortable today. Let's save it for when we can really enjoy it."

"I suppose you're right," Philippa muttered, "but— crikey!—the two of you can be so *maddeningly* sensible." She stalked into the house, feigning disgust, but turned around in the doorway to say, "Danny, I think I do need some water now. And Lark, I suppose you'd better set the table in that *ghastly* dining room."

But on this day even the dining room seemed bright, and breakfast was one of the most cheerful meals they had had in the house. Needless to say, Philippa understood that this was a special day, and to Danny's surprise actually encouraged Lark to miss school, just this once. "After all," she said, "I wouldn't want to be the cause of your wasting a single minute of this glorious weather in some dull old classroom."

After they had cleaned up, however, and Danny said, "Lark and I are going to walk over to the tumuli," Philippa's bright expression faded. "But, darling," she said, "I was thinking, since this weather has made us all feel so energetic, wouldn't it be a good time to whitewash the dining room? We've got to do it sometime, and since Lark *is* here today it will go all the faster. . . ."

There was nothing they could do. Philippa was determined to whitewash today, no matter what. "Even if I have to do it all myself," she said; and they certainly couldn't let her do that. Quickly they moved all the furniture out of the room. The polished oval table and ornately carved chairs were scattered haphazardly among the bushes and trees in the yard, looking stuffy and ill at ease, like overdressed people at the wrong party. Philippa took the canvas tarpaulin from Lil's engine (where she tucked it carefully every night to keep the car warm), and spread it over the dining room floor. The three of them began to paint. Though Lark and Danny painted furiously, in order to get it over with, they were obviously bored by the whole business. But Philippa seemed to love every minute of it. It's interesting, Danny thought (feeling very frustrated), how a day like this makes Lark and me long to be outside, but it makes *her* want to fix up the house.

The job took most of the day, for Philippa was a perfectionist about such things. They ate lunch outside, holding their sandwiches in raw, shaking hands, walking around the yard as they ate, to keep warm; occasionally sitting down for a moment on the fancy chairs. The chairs faced away from each other, and the three of them sat staring blankly off in different directions, chewing like cows on the thick sandwiches.

Then quickly back into the dining room, seeming all the darker now that they had been outside again. But whitewashing could be almost pleasant, Danny thought, particularly if there were a lot on your mind to mull over while your hand moved up and down. Naturally Danny concentrated on the tunnel.

Eventually, however, he began to notice a strange, tight feeling in his head. He had been so preoccupied, for so long, with the same dark imaginings. He longed to forget about it all, to let loose in openness and freedom and light. And he kept glancing toward the window, to the day that was moving inexorably into afternoon, and back to the gradually diminishing patch of unpainted wall.

At last they were finished, and there was still some daylight left. The cleaning up was maddening. They sped about, picking up the tarp, cleaning the brushes, putting things away, moving all the furniture back into the room.

Lark and Danny could hardly stop to admire their work as Philippa so blissfully was doing. Almost dancing in their eagerness, they began to edge toward the door, waiting for their chance to get away.

Suddenly Philippa turned toward them from where she was examining the wall. "You two certainly are in a hurry to get out of here," she said. "Are you up to something?"

"No," Danny said. "We just want to get to the tumuli before dark. We've been planning on it all day."

"It's interesting, Danny, the way you're always so energetic now, always up and about," she mused slowly. "You always used to be so comfortably lethargic, always sitting down whenever you had the chance. . . ."

"Was I?" he said impatiently, trying to be polite. "But I thought you didn't like it that I was lethargic, I thought you always wished I—"

"Oh, forget it. Yes, go on now. But *please* try to get back before dark." Nevertheless, Danny grabbed the large flashlight as they raced out the door.

They hardly spoke as they walked quickly down the track. The new feeling in the air was still as exciting as it had been that morning, especially after all the hours spent inside. The tightness in Danny's head began to melt away; the sunlight seemed to penetrate through his hair, smoothing out the tension and brushing away all the twisted, tangled thoughts.

Were they really walking faster and faster as they went on? Never had the different landmarks fallen behind so quickly. Before they knew it they were at the edge of the plateau, and there were the clouds speeding overhead, the hills and valleys falling all around them; and the three sloping mounds, tantalizingly ominous even on a day like this.

Why was the wind so different here, why did the clouds move so magically? They strolled across the brown grass, gazing off at the endless countryside that was clearer, closer today than ever before.

Danny grabbed Lark's hand as they ran up the nearest mound. Panting, they reached the top together.

"My God! What's that?" Danny cried.

Planted in the center of the flat space enclosed by the three mounds was a large pole, rising at least thirty feet into the air. It was a plain wooden pole, growing slightly thinner at the top; nothing but a tall tree stripped of bark and branches and sanded smooth.

Danny dropped Lark's hand and hurried down the mound to the base of the pole. It was perfectly smooth to his touch, and, in fact, was very beautiful, the dark pattern of the grain making intricate designs over the entire surface. He pushed it, but it was so deeply embedded in the ground that it would not move at all.

Lark joined him. "Well," she said, "I suppose it's obvious why this is here. They're going to have another one of those fire things up here."

"Yes." Danny was staring fixedly off into space. He sighed. "If only I could have heard them better!"

"Heard who?"

"Lord Harleigh and the librarian. But I do distinctly remember one of them saying something like 'getting closer and closer' . . . and it suddenly occurred to me just now, maybe *they're* mixed up in what you saw up here." He turned to face her. "Is there anyone else at all around here who is so strange and secretive?"

"Well, no . . ."

"And it might help to explain why they are so concerned about us being at Blackbriar. You know, I really do think I must be right."

"There's no proof."

"It seems so logical though. But of course there's nothing we can do about it anyway, whether I'm right or not. We'll just have to wait and see."

Aimlessly they wandered about the pole. "So it's really

going to happen again," Danny kept saying, almost to himself. Lark said nothing. This grim reminder seemed to sap away all the exuberance and joy they had felt only moments before. The tumuli were dismal now, and the wind was cold. Soon they started back.

"Isssslington!" they could hear Philippa calling as they neared the cottage, "Issssslington!" When they stepped out of the thicket of pines they could see her standing in the center of the yard, looking very distraught in the gathering dusk.

"Oh, there you are!" she said, running toward them. "You haven't seen Islington, have you? He's been gone all day. I was so preoccupied with painting that room that I forgot all about him. I haven't seen him since early this morning."

"I don't remember seeing him at all," Danny said.

"Neither do I," said Lark.

"He's *never* been gone this long before," Philippa moaned. "Oh, how could I have forgotten about him like that? The poor thing. Anything could have happened to him. He could be lost, or trapped somewhere, or . . ." and her voice almost broke, "something could have . . . got him. I know there are foxes around here, and perhaps even wolves." She turned away from them quickly. "Isslington!" she called again, hoarsely, "Issssssslington, darling, where are you?"

Lark and Danny glanced at each other. "I guess we should go look for him," Danny said. "He's probably just chasing something. Are you sure he's not in the house?"

"Yes, I've checked everywhere. I *know* something awful has happened, I just *know* it." She sounded hopeless.

"I wish I could help," Lark said hesitantly, "but I've really got to get back. My father must be worried by now. I'll walk down."

"No," Philippa said, "I'll drive you. Islington may have wandered down the road. Someone in the pub might have seen him. But you stay here, Danny, just in case he comes back."

Lark would rather have walked than ride with Philippa, who even in her best mood was never very friendly to her, but neither she nor Danny wanted to cross Philippa now. Soon the two of them were rumbling away down the track.

Danny stood in the doorway as the car noises grew fainter and finally disappeared. He called Islington's name a few times but soon stopped. His voice sounded ominous and lonely against the wind.

It was only a few minutes later that, still standing in the doorway, Danny noticed two glittering orange disks watching him from the darkness under the trees. "Islington?" he said. Cautiously he began to walk toward them.

The disks dissolved and Islington loped out of the woods. "Islington!" Danny cried, relief flooding through him like hot tea in his stomach. But at the sound of his name the cat froze, then took a step or two backwards. Danny stopped walking and watched, silently. After a moment Islington began to walk toward him again, but strangely. Something was different about the way he moved, but it was too subtle for Danny to tell what it was. When the cat came very close, Danny reached out to pet him. Islington growled and spat, his hair standing on end, and bit Danny's finger, drawing blood.

"Ouch! Damn you!" Danny cried, and began to suck on his finger. Islington hurried into the house.

At first Danny couldn't see the cat anywhere inside. He wasn't in his usual places by the fire or the stove.

But he found him at last in his own room. He was clawing violently at Danny's chest of drawers, shivering and making pitiful moaning noises.

"Now what are you doing *that* for, you nasty beast?" Danny said. And then he remembered what was hidden inside the dresser.

17

Philippa brooded silently over one cigarette after another as Danny bolted down his two eggs and three pieces of toast. He swallowed the last crust and hurriedly began clearing the table, balancing cups and plates on his arms to get it over with as soon as possible. He dropped them into the sink, then headed for the door.

"Danny," she said.

"What?" He paused restlessly in the dining room doorway.

"Sit down. We've got to talk."

He slumped into a chair, drumming on the table with his fingertips.

"I just can't stop thinking about Islington. You *must* tell me everything that happened. I can't *bear* to see him like this."

"But I told you everything, about ten times." He sighed

again, then began to speak with exaggerated patience. "He came out of the woods. He was walking strangely. He bit my hand when I tried to pet him. He went inside. You know all the rest, you came back right after that."

"Yes, but don't you have any idea what might have happened? Why, he doesn't eat, he won't even let *me* touch him, he doesn't hunt mice, he just moons around all the time. You must have some idea."

"But why should I know any more about it than you?" He shifted uncomfortably in his chair. "And I've got to go get some firewood."

"Well, if you don't know anything," she said, suddenly angry, "why do you keep trying to avoid my questions?" She stabbed out her cigarette and began fumbling for a new one.

"I'm not avoiding your questions. We just need some more firewood, that's all."

"Oh, don't give me that. I know you. I can tell when you're hiding something. And it's cruel, cruel of you to keep anything about Islington from me! *You've* changed as much as he has."

He stood up quickly, scraping back his chair. "I'm going outside, I can't take this anymore!" he shouted, and stormed out of the house.

Islington was standing in the yard, quivering and shaking helplessly. As Danny ran past, the cat howled and dashed away. He remembered how proud and brave Islington used to be; and even though he had always considered the cat obnoxious, now a sudden feeling of pity for the animal swept over him. He stopped and turned around to try and find Islington and comfort him, but then he remembered his anger at Philippa and continued on his way.

He walked quickly down the track. Instead of his coat, he wore a jacket and heavy sweater, for it was less cold today than ever. He could still see his breath, but his face did not sting, and as he walked quickly he began to feel warm.

And, of course, he did have ideas about what had happened to Islington. That part of the conversation in the library had been difficult to hear, but he had noticed how special they seemed to think Islington was, and with what glee they had discussed doing something to him. And whatever it was, Danny speculated, they must have done it.

He turned right, following a path into the woods on the side of the hill. But what could they have done to produce such an eerie change in Islington's behavior? There were no signs that he had been physically hurt in any way. And why should anyone *want* to do anything to a helpless cat? It just didn't make sense.

And, of course, he couldn't tell Philippa. Without knowing definitely that something had happened to him, she might eventually be able to convince herself that Islington was just going through some sort of phase, and stop worrying. But if she knew that someone had actually mistreated him deliberately she would be beside herself; she might even go to them and do something about it; she might even want to leave. It was better to prevent these possibilities. And this time, he reflected, he wasn't at all worried that she would succeed in prying it out of him.

The woods were mostly pine, and on this day the pathway

was flecked with brilliant patches of sunlight. The other trees were still bare, but there was so much green that it really didn't feel like winter at all. He began to walk more slowly, and soon stopped altogether. What was that noise, over to the left? It sounded a bit like the wind in the trees, but seemed to come from one particular spot. He left the path and began to walk through the trees, following the sound. There was no underbrush, the ground was covered with pine needles, and the trees were not very close together, so that he had no trouble making his way. The patches of sunlight danced when the wind blew.

The sound grew louder, more distinct. The ground began to slope steeply down, and soon he was sliding on the needles, grabbing trees for support.

At the bottom of the gully was a brook. Here, its sound was very loud, almost drowning out everything else. The water was perfectly clear, he could see the stony bottom, and it splashed and churned over mossy rocks, making small, foamy waterfalls. The sun sparkled on its surface. He squatted at the edge and dipped in his hand, then quickly pulled it out. The water was icy.

I've got to show this to Lark, he thought, as proud of his discovery as if he had made the brook himself. Do brooks come from springs? he wondered. Maybe I'll find the beginning if I follow it up the hillside. He stood up and started off along its edge. It was fascinating to watch the different waterfalls, the different patterns the brook made as it raced down the hill. As he went on, he saw places where the brook was fed by tiny trickles of water sliding down to it over slippery rocks. Occasionally he had to step from rock to rock in the brook itself, when there was no room to walk along the edge. It was cold under the trees, but the patches of sunlight were warm on his forehead.

The surrounding countryside soon became very familiar to him, for he began to spend as little time as possible at home. At night, however, he could not stay away—and at night he would lie awake and listen. Above the sounds of Philippa tossing in bed, above the sound of her snores, he listened for noises from the basement, or at the cellar door. He heard the creaking of the house, and the wind and the rain, and the scuffling of all the mice that Islington no longer chased. But from the tunnel there was an ominous silence.

When he slept, he dreamed, always. And the dreams were the same, but more terrifying, more real. The room was longer, the window farther away, the bodies were warm and clutched him more roughly. And he waited, as he struggled through them, for the laughter that would end the dream. For the laughter was familiar, almost comforting now, and he longed for it to last as it faded away in the darkness . . .

"What were you and Lark doing while I was at the hair-dresser's that day?"

Danny set down his glass of milk. "Nothing."

"You must have been doing *some*thing."

"I don't know. What difference does it make? It took us a long time to walk up here, then we lit the lamps and built the fires and everything, and . . . went for a little walk, then we just sat by the fire and talked."

"What did you talk about?"

"I don't *remember*. Nothing important. Why does it matter so much?"

"It matters so much because you've been different lately. You were both different that night. As though you were hiding something. What did she tell you?"

"Nothing!"

Philippa pushed away her half-eaten lamb chop and lit a cigarette. "I wonder if we ever should have come here at all. It's changed you. And that girl's been part of it. I should have known what she was like. She's made you secretive and two-faced."

"She has not. We're just friends. What's wrong with that?"

"Everything in her case. I don't want you seeing her anymore."

"How interesting. But *I* happen to want to see her, and I don't care what you say. And may I ask what's so terrible about her?"

"Look at the way she's been brought up. No mother, an irresponsible artist for a father—"

"What makes you think he's irresponsible?"

"—traipsing in and out of that pub whenever she likes, going to that awful country school, never learning any manners."

"She always helps out when she's here."

"Well, she's not coming here anymore."

"But what has she done?"

"You two have secrets. I'm sure you know something

about this house that I don't know. I'm sure you know something about poor Islington. *She* must know about Lord . . . Lord Barley, or whatever his name is, she's been living here for so long. *Why* do you have to keep secrets from me?"

"But I don't know any more than you."

"Then why do you always make sure the cellar door is latched before you go to bed?"

"Do I?" he said, taken aback. He hadn't realized she had noticed. "I don't know why. Because that basement scares me, I suppose. You know I've always thought it was creepy down there."

"Oh, you may be very glib, but I know you're keeping something from me, and I can't bear it. I won't allow it!"

"Look," Danny said, strangely calm, "I am getting very tired of the way you constantly pick at me and tell me what to do and pry into every little corner of my life. And no matter what you say, I'm simply not going to put up with it anymore. There's no reason in the world why I should let you treat me this way. Do you want the rest of your lamb chop?"

For a moment, Philippa gazed blankly at him with her mouth half opened, and it suddenly dawned on Danny what he had just said. His natural impulse was quickly to say something that would soften the impact of his words; but before he had a chance to think what he might say, Philippa rose from the table. "Here," she said, pushing her plate toward him, "take it." And, almost as if she had been hit, she stumbled from the room.

18

And then, picking up firewood one afternoon, he noticed something green starting to push its way up out of the ground. It was only the smallest beginning of a leaf, but he had been waiting so long for something like this that he was suddenly bursting to tell someone. As he hurried back to the house he felt a quick wave of compassion for Philippa. Maybe this will make her feel better, he thought, she *has* been having it pretty rough lately.

"Guess what?" he called as he staggered inside and dropped the wood in a heap on the hearth. "Guess what I saw in the woods?"

There was no answer.

Oh, God, is she still sulking? he thought. "Hey, I have some good news," he called again. "Philippa?" He noticed that she hadn't lit the fire, which was odd. It was usually blazing when he got back with the wood. And one of the chairs was pushed back from the hearth, wrinkling the rug underneath it.

In the kitchen, there was a pan of potatoes on the oil stove, but no flame under them. The fire in the coal stove was almost out.

"Philippa!" he called again. She never lets the stove go out, he thought, and suddenly he felt afraid.

He ran up the stairs two at a time. The second floor was as empty as the first. He started to call her name again, from her bedroom, but stopped. His mind filled with all kinds of possibilities. She's probably just gone for a walk, he told himself.

The sun was setting, and her room was becoming very dark. Outside, the car sagged tiredly at the edge of the woods. He had never felt so alone. I've got to light the lamps all by myself, he thought idly. Now there was only one more place to look.

Downstairs, he took the flashlight from its kitchen shelf. He didn't want to turn it on, because that would mean it was truly night now; but when he reached the cellar door his finger moved almost automatically. "Mary Peachy" stood out in the sudden oval of light, and trying not to think, he quickly pulled open the door.

He kept his mind a blank as he walked slowly down the damp steps, not wanting them to end. He stopped on the last step and flashed his light into the corner.

The bedspring had been pushed away and was lying flat on the floor about three feet from the wall. The little door hung loosely on its hinges. Numbly, he walked across the room. Lying just outside the passageway, on the cellar floor was a silver chain. It was Islington's collar.

"Oh, no," he said aloud. "Oh, no. Why was I so stupid, why, why, why?" He closed his eyes and let the flashlight dangle from his hand. "Why?" he moaned again. Almost as clearly as if he had been there, he imagined Philippa and Islington being dragged through the door. Did she fight? Were they rough? Did they have to knock her out? He put his hand over his eyes and shook his head slowly back and forth. And what was happening to her now?

There was a sudden, loud banging on the front door.

He almost dropped the flashlight. And truly unable to think, to imagine who it could be, he dashed up the steps, through the dark living room, and swung open the door.

A policeman stood there, and a man in a gray business suit. Danny's immediate relief at seeing a policeman at this particular moment was followed at once by the fear that he must have some terrible news about Philippa. And the man in the suit, why was he so strangely, distantly familiar?

"Mr. Daniel Chilton?" the policeman said. The man in the suit was staring at Danny.

"What happened?" Danny gasped.

"*You* are the one who knows that, I'm afraid," said the man, drawing his heavy brows together.

"What? What do you—?" But suddenly Danny realized who the man was, and his heart sank. "Oh," he said quietly, "hello, Mr. Bexford."

"May we come in, please?" said the lawyer. "This has been quite a trip, I must say." He peered inside. "Why are there no lights on? And where is Mrs. Sibley, may I ask?"

"Oh," Danny said again, now at a total loss for words. He thought of the chair pushed back by the hearth, of the open door in the basement and the fallen bedspring. "I haven't had time to light the lamps yet. And Philippa isn't here. She—went to the hairdresser."

"I see," Mr. Bexford said. His voice was shaking. "She *walked* all the way down the hill from this primitive, god-forsaken hole and into Dunchester. Or has she acquired two Land Rovers since I last heard from you?"

"I—she—we like to walk. It's healthy. That's one of the reasons why we came here, so we could walk, and be in the country, and—"

"That madwoman!" He turned to the policeman, who seemed somewhat taken aback. "How inconceivably irresponsible to bring a child out to a place like this. Why, it's incredible, it's—"

"Now wait a minute," Danny said. "She's *not* irresponsible, she just thought—"

"But where is she, young man? It's her responsibility to take care of you, you know."

"She really is at the hairdresser," Danny insisted. "She should be back soon . . ." How warm it is tonight, Danny thought. He was still standing in the open doorway, and could feel himself beginning to sweat.

"As a matter of fact, I don't really give a damn where she is," Mr. Bexford was saying. "This is the end, as far as I'm concerned. The end. I'm going to get you away from her so fast you won't know what's happened. And *don't* you dare contradict me! It *is* irresponsible to take a child away from school and out to a place like this. What do you know about such things anyway?"

"I'm sorry," Danny said, trying to think what would be the best thing to say, and knowing that he had to be polite. "It's just that . . ." How awkward it feels to be standing in the doorway, he thought. But I can't let them in. And then he noticed something strange far over to the right, above the trees. "It's just that I think you're mistaken about her, sir. I've passed my 'O' levels, and she thought a holiday in the country would be good for me. And I've been studying . . . I feel much better here—"

"I don't want your flimsy excuses. I just want you to pack your things and come with me, right now."

"Now? But I can't!"

"What do you mean, you can't? Why can't you?"

"I . . . I just can't. I . . . there's something I have to do."

"What do you *have* to do that could possibly be more important than coming back with me, getting your finances in order, and enrolling in a decent school? The more you balk, you know, the worse it's going to be for you."

"Please, *please*," Danny begged. "Just let me stay a few more days, one more day, just till tomorrow. I've *got* to!" Yes, there was definitely a strange light, a bit like sunset, over there above the trees. But the sun has already set, he thought, and that isn't west anyway.

"I'm sorry, young fellow," the policeman was saying, "but I have instructions to bring you back with him. I think you'd better get moving now."

Almost frantic, Danny suddenly remembered a distant television show. "Do you have a warrant?" he said.

"Well, no, I don't, we didn't expect—"

"Then, please," Danny said, "both of you, go away."

"What?" Mr. Bexford gasped.

"Just go away!" Danny cried, and slammed the door in their faces.

He backed up and leaned against the wall as they pounded on the door. "Come out!" Mr. Bexford cried. "I'm your legal guardian, you impudent little monster! Do you dare tell us to go away? Do you dare?"

"Sir," the policeman said gently, "I'm afraid there's nothing we can do. It is the lady's house, you know, she's signed the lease, we've seen the document, and we can't break in without a warrant."

"We'll be back!" Mr. Bexford shouted. "As soon as we get that warrant we'll drive right back up this hill—"

"But perhaps not tonight," the policeman interrupted in a loud whisper. "They might not want us to take the car up again tonight, it's not that urgent. It's not as if he was a criminal, you know."

"We'll be back!" Mr. Bexford cried. "You won't get away from me again!" Muttering, they moved away. Danny heard a motor starting up, wondering why he hadn't heard it before, and listened to it grow fainter as it bumped off down the hill.

And then he paced the floor in the dark room, the flashlight still glowing in his hand. He paced the floor and tried to organize the thoughts that were spinning through his head. He had to forget about these men and try to figure out what to do about Philippa. The tunnel, should he go through the tunnel, did he have to go through the tunnel?

He stopped. What was that noise? Where was it coming from? His teeth were chattering uncontrollably. It didn't sound as if it were coming from the tunnel. And then he remembered the strange light he had seen, off above the tumuli.

He raced to front door and peered outside. Far off to the right the jagged black shapes of the trees were outlined against a red glow. Swirling smoke was disappearing into the dark sky. A hollow, rhythmic beat floated through the stillness, faintly filling the deserted yard. The birds were silent, and even the wind seemed to have stopped. The only sounds were the deep, pulsing beats, and occasional, almost inhuman cries.

For a moment he stood motionless in the doorway. The rhythm seemed to fill his head, to push out everything but its beckoning, mesmerizing call. He struggled against it, and finally tore himself back into the house and slammed the door. But it was hardly better inside. The drumbeats penetrated through the thick stone walls, and as he paced about in the dark room the house itself seemed to become part of the rhythm. He tried to think, to see his situation clearly, to decide what to do. But he could only wander helplessly around the room and watch the bizarre, terrifying images that raced through his head to the rhythm of the drums.

How long he remained like this he didn't know. Perhaps it was only a short while, but to him it seemed a timeless hell. He cursed himself for not telling the truth to the policeman. He cursed himself for not running immediately into the tunnel. But perhaps it was a trap. Perhaps Philippa was dead.

Finally there was the sound of light footsteps outside, of a hesitant knock. It was the most refreshing sound he had ever heard. Not caring who it was, just so long as it would end this awful time, he flung open the door.

He was blinded by a bright flashlight beam. "Danny!" Lark gasped. "You look *awful*! What have you been *doing*?"

"Oh, God," he said, "thank God you came."

And while Danny talked, breathlessly, ceaselessly, Lark darted inside, began lighting candles, and by the time he had finished there was a small, bright fire and they were both holding steaming cups of tea. And the drumbeats, though still audible, were distant now, somewhere far away, outside the house.

"I don't know what was wrong with me," he groaned, "I couldn't think or do anything. I just wandered around so stupidly. Those drums got inside of me. I must have wasted so much precious time, with Philippa probably in some terrible situation, and it's all my fault."

"I don't think it was that long," she said gently. "I *raced* up here as soon as I noticed the first fire, and it couldn't have taken me more than half an hour. And don't keep saying it's all your fault; we both thought it was better not to tell her, and who expected them to take her away?"

"But we've got to act fast," Danny said. Was it the hot tea that made him feel suddenly in control of the situation? "The most important thing is what is happening to Philippa. Obviously, she's got to be wherever the tunnel goes to—which is probably Harleigh Manor, right?"

"Everything seems to point to that, and I can't think of anywhere *else* it could possibly go."

"And it seems to me that Lord Harleigh, and whoever else he's involved with, must have some relation to whatever is going on at the tumuli now. I mean, it would be too much of a coincidence for them to take Philippa away on the same night if they had no connection to it."

"Unless, of course, they were hoping it would take attention away from what they were doing."

"Oh." For a moment, Danny's newly formed, logical plan seemed to disintegrate. "Oh. That changes things. Because I was assuming that whoever is usually at Harleigh Manor would be over at the tumuli now, and that we could slip in through the tunnel and look for Philippa without anyone noticing. But . . ." The image of Philippa being dragged through the tunnel flashed through his mind again, and he knew that there was no time to hesitate. "But it doesn't matter *who's* there. We've got to go and look for her. I mean, we've got to, there's nothing else we can do."

Lark stood up. "I know, I know," she said, setting down her cup and folding her hands together nervously. "I knew when I came up here that we were going to have to do something. But somehow I didn't expect—I didn't think that somebody's *life* would depend on it." She was staring off into the dark side of the room. "And . . . and I thought we were going to be outside, not all closed up in some horrible dark place. I think I'm going to need a lot of help from you."

"I know." He stepped quickly over to her and put his

hand on her shoulder. The fire was beginning to die out, and the room was growing very dark again. "We've got to get going," he said softly.

In a moment he was upstairs, holding a candle, fishing about in his drawer. Lark was waiting with a flashlight when he returned with the wooden figure in his hand. "Why are you bringing *that*?" she said.

"I don't know. I just feel I should. I don't know why."

He slipped the wooden figure into his jacket pocket and pulled open the cellar door.

19

Danny led the way down the cellar steps and crawled in through the little doorway ahead of Lark. When they reached the place where they could stand they walked side by side, each with a flashlight. Down the steps they wound, not speaking a word. The distant drumbeats faded while around them the cold and the dampness grew, and the echoes of their footsteps, and the sound of dripping water. At the landing, neither looked into the room with the bones, and hardly pausing, they started down the long flight.

It was an odd sensation not to be able to see the end, only more steps far, far below in the pale circles of their lights. It was almost as though there were nothing beneath them, that if they should slip they would simply fall through empty space. Lark held tightly to Danny's arm. As they continued, they began to go more slowly. The steps were slippery and uneven, and became narrower as they descended.

The silence was so complete that every footstep seemed to reverberate through the entire passage, above and below, as though there were others on the stairs.

Soon the house above seemed miles and miles away, tiny and unreal. Their legs ached from constantly stepping down. Strange thoughts began to creep into Danny's head. Perhaps the steps ended at a blank wall, or stopped in midair at the brink of an endless void, or led deep down into the earth to some horrifying other world. It came to him then that today was the first time in many weeks that he had had such thoughts; before, he had had them all the time. He struggled to push the thoughts away but it was hard because there was nothing but darkness all around them. Perhaps it would never end at all and they would just keep going down and down forever, two tiny lights descending eternally in the blackness.

Both lights were pointed at their feet now. It had become too disheartening to watch the distant steps keep appearing below them as they went on and on. And that is why the shock was so great when they stepped forward and suddenly found themselves on a level surface.

They both stumbled and almost fell. "Oh!" Lark said. "My God, I thought that was never going to end!" It was the first thing either of them had said since they had left the house, and the sound of her voice was like a bright light in the darkness.

"So did I! I kept thinking all these crazy things." He laughed shakily. "I'll bet those steps seemed much longer than they really are." He pointed his light back up the steps, and could clearly see the landing at the top, not so very far away. He walked around in a small circle. "But it certainly feels good not to step down."

"Wait," she said quickly, "don't get too far away." She moved close beside him. Standing together, they flashed their lights about them. They were in a rough passageway, the stone walls and ceiling jagged and unfinished. Boards had been laid along the bottom of the tunnel, and water was seeping up between them. Ahead, the tunnel curved off to the right.

"Wet down here," Danny said. Great clouds of steam came from his mouth.

"Yes."

"Well, let's go."

The boards were slippery, but much better going than the steps. Although the tunnel seemed to be heading in one general direction, it curved slightly, one way and then another, as though whoever had made it had only haphazardly planned the route. It was impossible to see more than a few feet ahead. The dripping was all around them, and little icy droplets fell continually onto their heads. They slowly plodded onward, unable to guess how long it would be, not speaking, not looking behind. It was very cold.

Suddenly Danny noticed that Lark had been gradually walking more slowly, hanging onto his arm, so that now they were proceeding at about half their original pace.

"Hey," he said, turning to her, "what's wrong?" He could only see her face dimly in the reflected light from his flashlight.

"I—I don't know." She shook her head. "It's like I'm slowly getting paralyzed, or something. It's hard to make myself move, I just want to stop."

"But why?"

"I think—it's being in this tunnel." They had stopped walking and she was looking around frantically at the walls and ceiling. "I hate this!" she cried suddenly. "I can't *bear* it in here! We've got to get out, Danny."

"But we're almost there, I'm sure."

"But . . . I don't know how much longer I can keep going."

"Come on," he said, "don't think about it," and pulled her roughly and started walking at a quick pace again. She stumbled along behind, looking up at the ceiling. The muscle in her arm was tight and quivering.

"Don't look up!" Danny said, glancing back at her. "Just look straight ahead, or else close your eyes. I'll guide you." When is this thing going to end? he wondered. Lark's eyes were tightly closed, she was stumbling, slowing him down considerably. Maybe I shouldn't have brought her, he thought. And what if the door at the other end is locked? I never thought of that. We'd have to go all the way back, she'd never make it. And what about Philippa then?

Lark stopped so suddenly that his hand jerked right out of hers.

"Lark?" he said. "Lark? Come on, we're practically there." He gave her arm a gentle tug but she resisted it. He sighed and dropped his hand.

"I can't go any farther," she said softly. "I just can't make myself move." Her head was down and her eyes still seemed to be closed. "You go on. I'm staying here."

"But you can't! How will you ever get out? Don't be so stupid! Just come *on*."

"No!"

"Oh, God," Danny sighed. He turned and faced ahead. "Now what do I do?" he said.

"Just go on," she murmured.

He groaned. And then he looked ahead more closely. Was that a light? He switched off his flashlight. There was a dim glow coming from around the bend just ahead. "Lark!" he cried, "Lark, open your eyes! There's a light! Just around the corner." She looked up. "See? Now you can make yourself move. Come on!" He grabbed her hand and began to run. She slipped and almost fell but he did not stop, and she staggered along behind him. They turned the corner, and ahead they saw the remains of a stone wall, part of which had been knocked away to make an entrance. The light was coming from behind it.

They stumbled through the wall. Lark moaned with relief. They were in a room. On the wall beside them was another torch in a bracket. Lark leaned against the stone wall and rested her head against it, looking up. "Oh," she started to say, "what a—"

"Shhh!" Danny was looking around them. Across from where they stood was an ascending flight of stone steps.

"Do you think this is Harleigh Manor?" Lark whispered.

"We'll find out soon enough." He started toward the stairs, then turned back to her. "Remember, we've got to be as quiet as possible, there's probably somebody here."

At the top of the stairs was a heavy black metal door, tightly closed. Danny touched it gingerly, but it did not move. They glanced at each other for a moment, realizing that any noise could be disastrous. But if they could not open the door, there would be nothing to do but go back through the tunnel. It occurred to Danny that that might be the best thing after all.

He pushed again, with more force. Still the door would not move. He looked at the latch. Should I try it? he wondered. What about the noise? But he couldn't think. With Lark's heavy breathing beside him he grasped the latch and pushed down the catch with his thumb. There was a click. Then slowly, carefully, he began to push the door. It moved, silently. He pushed faster, faster, and there was a sudden squeak and a heavy scraping sound and he whipped his hand back to his side. His heart was pounding in his neck.

They waited, listening, but even after their hearts had quieted they could not hear a sound. The opening was still just a little too narrow to squeeze through, so in a moment Danny's hand crept back to the latch. He pushed again, very slowly, and the door squeaked and scraped but his hand kept moving, even as Lark clutched at his arm with sharp nails. When the opening was just wide enough he stopped, turned to look at Lark, then stepped through the door. She followed quickly.

A foul smell greeted them. They were standing in a dimly lit kitchen, and as they waited just inside the door, motionless and listening, Danny's eyes moved quickly. A candle, fastened by its own wax to a table in the center of the room, cast its struggling light over an array of dusty, haphazard objects on sagging shelves: glass bottles containing small bits of herbs and leaves, rusty iron implements he could not recognize, an empty whiskey bottle lolling carelessly on a tarnished silver platter. Everywhere there were plates with the remains of food still on them. At first the house seemed to be silent, but as they stood there they began to hear gentle creaks, and what were perhaps vague footfalls, filtering down from above.

They waited, but none of the sounds grew into anything definite, so soon Danny began to move. Beside the candle was a large mortar and pestle, still holding some strong-smelling herb. The surface of the table, really a large chopping board, was indented and scarred; strewn across it were old pieces of fat and bone, and several rusty knives and cleavers. Danny wondered if he should take one, but the idea of actually using it was unthinkable. Lark followed him; he stepped past the sink. It had no faucets, only a pump, and was filled with more food-encrusted dishes, some of which seemed to have been there for quite a while. They glanced at each other, and Lark grimaced and held her nose.

Danny pushed open the swinging door a crack, peered through, then they stepped into the next room. He turned back for a moment to be sure the door would close quietly— and suddenly Lark gave a terrified squeal and grabbed his arm.

Two eyes were staring at them. A lethal-looking chande-lier, holding a few feebly sputtering candles, barely illuminated the full length of a long banquet table. But they could very clearly see the pair of glassy eyes at the other end.

Trembling, they stood and simply stared into the eyes, which, continued to gaze placidly back. Why doesn't he say something? Why doesn't he say something? Danny screamed inside himself. But all at once Lark gave a strange sort of sigh, dropped her arm, and rushed straight at the eyes.

Maybe it's someone she knows, was his first thought. But the eyes ignored her, staring at him; and then Lark actually smiled and beckoned. He approached her carefully, and the shape around the eyes became the carcass of a large pig, bits of moist flesh still clinging to its empty ribs.

For a moment they clutched each other in relief. They were both still trembling. Danny pulled away first. Down the length of the table lay the remains of a feast. Greasy plates and cups and silverware, stained, crumpled napkins, fruit peel, sodden bits of puddings, cigarette and cigar ends embedded in pools of gelatinous gravy . . . It made him feel rather ill. He rested his hand on the back of a chair, and noticing the unusual texture, looked down. He quickly drew his hand away. It was exactly the same as the chairs at Blackbriar.

Lark had turned from the table and was peering behind the black velvet curtains that hung against one wall. They concealed a row of French windows looking out onto a moonlit garden, neglected and growing wild. It was a relief to see the outside again, but she felt something very close to hatred for anyone who would so deliberately hide from the out-of-doors.

A wide archway led from this room into a cramped front hall, where a narrow stairway rose dimly to the second floor. They paused, undecided about where to go. Danny began to notice creaks again. And then, distinctly, they heard a footstep above them.

Danny could barely see Lark's worried face. He motioned to her, and they moved past the stairs into the large room that lay across the hall from the dining room. A bit of gray light from one window made visible the crowded, indifferent furniture, the moth-eaten rug, old cabinets of books, and in a large pot in a corner, the dusty, twisted skeleton of a long dead plant. Danny bent close to Lark's ear and whispered, "There's nothing down here. We've got to go upstairs."

Lark frowned and shook her head. "Didn't you hear that footstep?"

"Yes, but we have to find Philippa. That's the only place left. And if somebody *is* up there, that's where Philippa's likely to be."

The first step creaked so loudly that Danny instantly stepped down. But there was no alternative, and trying to make as little noise as possible, they crept up the stairs. The railing was missing rungs in many places, and swayed under the pressure of Danny's hand. Paper was peeling off the wall beside them in long strips, exposing crumbling plaster beneath.

Just as he stepped onto the second floor, Danny heard footsteps again, and what could have been a moan. He turned to face Lark. She was shaking her head furiously, and pointing down the stairs. "No!" he hissed. "Come on. The footsteps are still above us. We're as safe here as we were downstairs."

Pale yellow light was coming from an open doorway opposite the stairs. He moved toward it cautiously and poked his head just inside. More black velvet covered all the walls except for one place across from him, where, in a large niche, surrounded by burning candles, stood a painting with a metal plaque beneath it.

There was no one in the room, and, less cautious now,

they moved toward the picture. It was a portrait of a young woman. She was dressed all in black, in seventeenth-century clothes. The style was primitive. Her clothing was stiff, with awkward folds; her hair looked like metal springs; her hands were wooden. But the artist had somehow managed to capture a real expression on her face, an expression of lively but suppressed amusement. She looked as though she were trying not to laugh.

In her hand she held the same wooden doll that Danny, who had unconsciously reached into his pocket, now had in his. And at the top of the plaque was the name, MARY PEACHY.

THE MANOR

20

Danny laughed. He tried desperately to hold the laughter in, so that it came out like a garbled cough, but for a full minute he could not stop. "Stop it!" Lark hissed. "Stop it, Danny!" and she covered his mouth with her hand.

He pushed her hand away. "Oh," he sighed, "why do I feel so happy? It's like I found a long-lost friend or something."

"Shut up!" She glanced behind her. "You're giving us away!"

"I'm sorry," he whispered, "I can't help it." He turned to read the inscription on the plaque:

MARY PEACHY

Born, 1645, Dunchester. Held in suspicion, fear, and hatred by the towns-people for her activities as a Witch. Tried and convicted in 1665 for bringing down the wrath of God in the form of the Great Plague, for her unholy activities. Though healthy, sentenced to imprisonment in the town pesthouse with the diseased. Remained in perfect health, though all the others eventually died. Continued to live alone at Blackbriar for the rest of her life. Left in peace by the townspeople, who no longer came near her. Date of death unknown.

"A witch!" Lark gasped.

The heavy curtains moved slightly, and Danny felt the wind on his neck. "Wait a minute," he said slowly. "This must mean . . . it must mean Lord Harleigh, and the others—"

"Are witches!"

"Or think they are. No wonder! No wonder they don't want us at Blackbriar. It must be like a shrine or something. And my God! that laughter . . ." He seemed to hear it in his head as he looked at the flat, pretty girl. Her eyes watched him as though they knew just what he was thinking, and were laughing. But she couldn't have been like Lord Harleigh, he thought, she must have been a good witch.

"The doll," Lark was saying. "It must be some kind of witch thing. No wonder Philippa hated it so. I wonder what it's suppposed to do?"

Danny held it up to the light. There was no doubt that it was the same doll, only more worn and smooth, as though many other hands had stroked it since the girl had held it in hers. He shivered, but he tightened his fingers on it. "I don't know what they think it does," he said, "but whatever it's for, I'm glad I have it, and not Lord Harleigh. It belongs to me now. Somehow . . . it makes me feel as though I can be as independent as Mary Peachy was."

Lark was watching him. "You frighten me," she said, even more softly. "It's almost as though, since you had it in your room for so long, and you kept hearing that laughter, Mary Peachy might have some kind of power over you."

Danny did not answer. Just above their heads the footsteps began again, rapidly, as though someone were pacing the floor. He tore his eyes away from the painting and hurried out into the dark second-floor hall.

This was a long, narrow corridor with doors on either side. Through an open one he could see only the vague shape of a large sagging bed with a canopy. Lark emerged from the candlelit room as Danny stood, debating whether to try all the doors or to head for the next floor, and the footsteps.

"What are you going to do now?" Lark whispered.

"I don't know. We've got to hurry." He turned his head quickly from side to side. "I guess we *should* try these doors."

He started down the corridor, peering through the open doors, carefully trying the closed ones. After he had tried two or three, Lark began too, on the other side of the hall. None of them were locked, and there seemed to be no one in any of the rooms. Are we wasting time? Danny worried. He knew he was putting off the moment when they would have to confront whatever was making the footsteps. And maybe Philippa wasn't even here, but somewhere else, in danger. And at any moment, Lord Harleigh might return.

Just as he had decided that it was useless to keep trying these empty rooms, he pulled open a door at the end of the hall, to find a steep, narrow stairway. Slowly, his eyes followed it up into complete darkness. He craned his neck forward and listened. Yes, the footsteps were definitely coming from somewhere at the top of the stairs.

Lark was standing just behind him. "All right," he whispered, "we've got to do this. Here we go."

He turned on his flashlight and started up the stairs. One step at a time, very, very slowly. He had learned that the only way to do something like this was simply not to think, not to try to imagine what was about to happen, but just keep moving. Like not looking down when you're climbing a tree, he thought. He reached a small landing, the stairs turned, and he saw that they ended at a closed door. Light was coming through the cracks around it; behind the door the footsteps were continous now, and very close. He still could not tell if they were the sounds of one person or two.

He turned off his light and started very quietly toward the door. Even more slowly, letting his foot come gently to rest on each stair before putting his weight on it. Behind him, Lark was moving so carefully that he hardly knew she was there.

And then there was a splintering sound and a heavy thud and a loud gasp of pain. He spun around. "What—?"

Lark was sprawled across three or four steps. She looked up at him, her hair in her eyes. Slowly she struggled to her feet. Danny listened. The pacing behind the door had stopped.

"That's super," he whispered angrily. "You've given us right away."

"Oh, shut up! I couldn't help it. The step broke." She sighed. "And my foot hurts."

"Well . . ." Danny turned back. He had reached the door. There was a key in the lock. The silence behind the door was ominous, worse than the footsteps had been. But there was only one thing to do. Without knowing why, he pulled the doll out of his pocket and held it in front of him. Then he took a deep breath, turned the key, and pushed open the door.

It was an attic room with steeply slanting walls. And just across from him, alone, Philippa was cringing as if to ward off a blow. Danny stepped inside, the fear on Philippa's face dissolved into relief, and she lunged toward them with open arms. "Oh, you darling, darling children!" she cried, and threw her arms around them both.

21

In a moment Philippa backed away and began to babble. "They took Islington. He fought and fought but they took him away and left me here. You darling things, how did you find me? I don't know what they're going to do with him, the poor little thing. He hated them so! But I don't understand any of this. What are they trying to do? Why did they take me here? Poor Islington! What are they doing with him?"

Lark and Danny watched her silently as she stumbled about the room. Her hair was tangled, her cheek bruised, and there was a long gash running up the side of her skirt. The only furniture in the room was a chair, and a table with a lighted candle. There were several small dormer windows in steeply pitched alcoves, and a profusion of boxes and trunks along the walls.

Gradually Philippa calmed down and finally sank into

the chair. "Yes," she said slowly, "how *did* you know I was here?"

"Well," said Danny, "you weren't at home and the car was there, and there were certainly signs that the tunnel had been used—"

"Yes!" she interrupted. Suddenly her voice was bitter. "The tunnel. And just how long have you *known* about that tunnel, you clever boy? And why didn't you *tell* me about the tunnel, you little bastard!"

"Please," Danny said, "don't get upset *now*. I just thought it was best. I thought you'd want to leave if I told you about it. I was only trying to protect—"

"Protect me? You call *this* protecting me?" She grabbed her bloody cheek and shook the skin at him. "It's protecting me to let me stay in a house that's wide open to a pack of brutal, sadistic, animal-torturing monsters?"

"Oh, God," Danny sighed. "Do we have to go through all this? Why can't we just calmly—"

"Danny," Lark interrupted from one of the windows, "look over there."

In the moonlight, the tumuli seemed very close. The fires on the three mounds and around the pole were brilliant against the dark sky. Undulating silhouettes moved wildly around them, and they could clearly hear the violent rhythm of the drums.

"Oh. I almost forgot," Danny said. He turned to Philippa. "I'm sure that's where Islington is. It must be some kind of witch festival, and I suppose they're using him in it."

"Do you think they might . . . sacrifice him?" Philippa whispered hoarsely.

"I don't know. I can't imagine what they want him for. But that's why they brought you here, you know, so that you wouldn't be in the way. And they probably do all these secret things that they don't want anyone to see. I wonder why they didn't wait to take me too?"

"They were going to," Philippa said. "I told them you had gone back to London."

"You *did*? You told them that? It's a good thing." He paused. "But what *happened* to you? Tell us exactly what happened."

Philippa sighed. "I had just finished peeling the potatoes. Poor Islington was pacing around. Then I heard this tremendous crash in the cellar, I couldn't imagine what it was, but before I had time to think they were racing up the stairs and into the living room—"

"Was the cellar door locked?"

"No, I'd gone down a while before to get some coal and I must have left it open. They *raced* into the room—"

"Who were they?"

"Well, there was a dwarf, and a tall fellow with dark hair, and this awful muscular woman who was about six feet tall. It was just the three of them, but they were all strong. The dwarf grabbed Islington and the woman held me down while the young man ran about looking for you. I kept saying you had gone back to London and in the end they believed me. Then they simply dragged me down the steps and into that tunnel, until I insisted on walking, and even then they never let go of my arms. They were terribly rough, and that woman stank horribly. Well, then we got to this house, and they immediately carted me up here, but the dwarf kept Islington. I kept yelling from the stairs, while they were hauling me up, for them to give him back to me, but of course they didn't. That little cat can really fight, though. The dwarf will never forget it; he'll bear those scratches to his grave. There was a lot of bustle in the house while they were taking me up, all sorts of bizarre characters running about. But after I'd been up here for a while it began to quiet down. I just stayed here, pacing the floor, and then I noticed the fires."

They could hear shouting from the tumuli. "I'm sorry," Danny said. "This *is* my fault. But I just wanted so much to find out what was really going on."

"Well, you should be bloody well satisfied now. By some miracle I'm not seriously injured, though, providing we can get out of here. But I suppose Islington's a lost cause."

"Not necessarily." Danny turned quickly to Lark. "Do you still want to go up there? How's your foot?"

"I forgot about it." She tested it on the floor. "It hurts a little, but I think it's all right. Of course I want to go up there. We've got to."

They stumbled together down the shadowy stairs, Philippa protesting weakly the whole time. "You can't go up there," she kept saying, "I won't allow it." They reached the hall and left the house by the front door. Briefly, they stood together on the doorstep.

"But what about Philippa?" Danny said. "She can't come with us."

"My house is right over there." Lark pointed across the road to a light in a small cluster of trees. "My father must

be home, he'll take care of you. I better not go with you,
though, he'd never let me go up to the tumuli tonight."

"But I won't let you, either," Philippa said.

"We've got to," said Danny. "We've gone this far, we
can't stop now. And we might be able to save Islington. Go
on, now, you need a nice hot bath."

Finally, Philippa stumbled off toward the light. They
stared after her for a moment, then turned to each other.
Danny took a deep breath. "Let's go," he said, and they
started up the hill.

22

The drumbeats seemed to pull them almost effortlessly up the steep slope, and as they neared the top the babble began to separate into distinct, hysterical voices. A strange, primitive melody rose and fell in counter-rhythm to the drums and stamping feet, and occasionally a single voice would rise above it all in a wordless cry. The three fires appeared first over the crest of the hill. A gaunt figure moved against the flames on the central mound.

They stopped. In the firelight they could clearly see the leering painted features on his oversized mask. The mask had horns.

Carefully Lark and Danny began to climb again. The tumuli rose to meet them, and the pole, with its own fire burning around it. And now, as they crouched at the edge of the plateau, thirty feet from the first mound, they could see the others. Perhaps forty people, both men and women, danced around the flames. The light flickered and splashed across the absorbed, upturned faces, the twisting bodies, the flashing hands. Some were old, with gray hair streaming out behind them. Some were beating on drums strung around their necks. Some, the young ones, threw themselves violently through the air in great, awkward leaps.

The dark plateau, the distant hills, the swollen moon hanging just above the horizon diminished the small bright circle, and seemed to watch it with boredom, as though they had seen the same thing many times before.

"What's that in his hands?" Lark whispered. "It moves!"

"Islington." Danny crawled forward, straining to see. He felt a familiar pang as he watched the cat writhe and twist in the masked figure's grasp. The man was trying to hold the cat above his head, as if to show it every detail of the activity below, but Islington seemed to hate the touch of his hands, and struggled painfully to get away.

"I've always hated Islington," Danny said.

"Hated him? But why?"

"I've always hated him, and I know just what it's like to try to hold him. But now, I can't bear to see him treated that way. It makes me so angry!"

"Shhhh! They'll hear us!" Lark crawled up next to Danny. "But what's he doing with him?"

"I don't know. I wish we could see better." Danny moved forward again. He felt protected by the darkness, and by the absorption of the dancing people. They appeared to be oblivious to everything but their own bodies, and the music, and the fires moving to the same rhythm. He moved up another few feet.

Lark followed him. "Don't get too close," she said. "We're close enough now."

But a strange recklessness moved inside him. "They'll never see us, they're not paying any attention to anything," he said sharply, and moved even closer to the first mound. His whole body seemed to be pulsing with the drumbeats; the bright violent movements flashed through his head.

Lark crawled up to him again, then looked back. She could just barely see the edge of the plateau behind them. They had come more than halfway across the open space between the hillside and the fires.

Suddenly there was a small dark shape in front of Danny, with two bright eyes. Something warm and soft pressed against his face.

"Islington!" He sat up. The cat burrowed into his stomach, crying and rubbing against him. Danny picked him up. "Islington, how did you—when did you get away?"

"Danny!" Lark screamed. "Look out!"

He glanced up. Everything was different. The people weren't dancing. They were running. They were running straight at him. And the masked figure was gone.

Lark was standing up, pulling at his arm. "Run, Danny!" she screamed.

He struggled to his feet. The people were all getting bigger and bigger, their faces growing clearer, the fires moving behind them. He held Islington tightly. He and Lark turned to run.

The figure sprang up from nowhere, his arms stretched out against the sky, his hideous face grinning and flickering.

They ran right into him. His hands clamped against their necks.

"Aha!" lisped the voice from the mask. "Two children. They have been watching us." He spun them roughly around to face the excited crowd clustered about them. "And how did you like what you saw, my two young spies?" All the eyes were on them, and the people were talking and whispering to each other. The dwarf was there, hopping about, and the tall, wiry young man who had built the fire at Blackbriar, but now his gaze was icy and calm. And was that the librarian, crouching and jiggling somewhere behind?

Danny struggled, but the grip tightened painfully on his neck. "I need your help!" the voice barked, and a hundred hands seemed to be holding him. He clung to Islington with all his strength; the mask swung before him now, and the powerful hands reached out for the cat.

"No!" Danny shouted. "You can't have him, you can't!" But the two hands were like iron, and they twisted and pried at the cat, and other hands pulled at Danny's arms, and he was powerless. Islington snarled and scratched out, but the man held him in one hand, high above his head.

"He belongs with us!" he cried. "He *is* one of us! It is he who led us to you. Let the festivities continue!" He marched back toward the fires, ahead of the crowd. Lark and Danny continued to struggle, but there were too many people all around them, and their efforts were useless. The leader turned as he reached the central mound. "The children," he said, "will come up here with me. You others can let them go. They know they will be caught if they try to run. And I don't think they want to leave their precious cat." Grandly, he climbed the mound.

The hands dropped away and the crowd quickly dispersed, as though they had already forgotten about Lark and Danny. The moment she was free Lark turned and ran, blindly. She was caught at once, kicking and twisting. "Unwise, my dear little girl," came the voice, "unwise. But now you know how futile any attempts at escape will be. Bring her to me."

Lark was hysterical. She tossed her head about and struggled uselessly. Danny was free now, and he hurried to her side, pushing his way through the three women who held her. He rested his hands on her shoulders. "Please," he said, "it's all right. We'll be better off if we do what he says." She stared at him blankly for a moment, then her face weakened, tears poured down her cheeks, and she leaned forward in heavy, painful sobs. It was Danny who led her up the mound.

Two small, mad eyes glared at them through the holes in the mask. "Do you know who this is?" The voice sounded hollow from behind the motionless mouth. He held the cat in front of him, not noticing Islington's busy claws and the blood dripping from his hands. "Do you know who this is? It is Belial, come to join us in our festivities."

"He's Islington," Danny said. "I recognize him. He knows me. He belongs to us."

"Perhaps he *was* Islington, once." The voice was shaking with excitement; firelight flickered in his eyes. "Perhaps. But now he is Belial, one of the most powerful fiends of Hell. We drew him here, from the other world, we drew him into the body of this cat."

"So you *did* have him that day we couldn't find him."

"And now he no longer belongs to any human being."

Below them the people had begun to dance once more. The music was inside Danny again, and he could hardly keep from moving in time. It filled his mind so that he couldn't think, any more than he could control his words.

"You must be crazy!" he shouted above the music. "You must be crazy to torture a poor cat and then think a devil is inside him!"

"Be careful, young man, be careful. You do not know to whom you speak."

"Of course I do. You're Lord Harleigh, anybody could recognize your voice, that silly mask doesn't disguise you one bit." Lark had stopped crying and was looking at Danny with surprise.

"Be quiet, you young fool! Tonight I am not any man. Tonight—I am the Evil One himself!" His voice rose triumphantly.

Danny snorted. Lark grabbed his jacket in an attempt to keep him quiet. The pocket had been torn in the struggle, and when she jerked the jacket something fell from the pocket to the ground at Danny's feet.

Lord Harleigh stepped back in amazement—and then moved quickly. But as his bloody hand touched the doll, Islington squirmed out of his grasp. He pounced at the cat, catching him just in time by the tail, and swung him into the air. "Got you!" he cried.

But Danny had the bloodstained doll.

"Where did you get that?" Lord Harleigh shrieked. "How did you find it? I thought it was gone forever. Give it to me!" He held Islington by his tail, and the cat wailed and twisted about. "Why did you bring it here? It's not yours. You have no right to it!"

"It belongs to me now!" Danny held it up. The doll's face was streaked with Lord Harleigh's blood. A strange idea leapt into Danny's mind.

"You must give it to me, you *must*!"

Was it fear shaking in his voice? Was Lord Harleigh afraid of the power of the doll? Danny clutched it tighter than ever.

Islington, who was still dangling, squirming in agony, suddenly swung himself over and dug deeply into Lord Harleigh's stomach, putting his whole weight into his claws. Lord Harleigh cried out, and instinctively flung the cat away from him.

Islington flew screeching into the fire.

Danny did not think. Holding his breath, his eyes wide open, he stepped into the flames. He heard Lark shriek and the music stop and his hair crackle, he felt the fire around him like boiling waves, and he saw Islington staggering and crying at the edge. He bent down, grabbed the cat by his withering fur, and stepped backwards, almost collapsing in the sudden coolness of the night air.

"Danny, Danny!" Lark was screaming. "Are you all right? Oh, your hair, your hair!"

He touched his head and felt the brittle strands crumbling to ash.

Lord Harleigh turned toward him from the fire. His whole body was shaking. It was not the cat he cared about now. "Give me that doll!" he shrieked, and lunged at Danny.

Danny thrust the whimpering cat into Lark's arms and darted away. Lord Harleigh could not see well, through the holes in the mask. He lunged at Danny again, and missed.

Danny held the doll above his head, dancing across the top of the mound. The people below watched silently, transfixed. "You'll never get it now," he cried. "I'm not afraid of you anymore. *You're* afraid of me!"

Grunting, Lord Harleigh ripped the mask from his head and tossed it aside. His face was long and pale, and twisted with fear and rage.

Danny danced away again as Lord Harleigh grabbed for him. "This doll is you now, isn't it! Isn't it! It has your blood on it. Whatever happens to it will happen to you. *That's* what you think it does! That's why you want it so much! Well, see how it feels!" he cried, and pitched the doll into the fire.

A cry of many voices rose from the people gathered below. Lord Harleigh stumbled. He raced to the fire and thrust in his arm, trying to reach the doll. But the fire was too hot for him, the doll was at the center of the blaze, and in a moment it was only a charred lump of wood. He turned to the people. "Help me!" he called. "Oh, help me! We shall burn them, as we have been burned!"

From all directions the crowd surged up the mound. No one noticed Islington now, and Lark held him tightly as she and Danny flew together and clutched each other in panic. Many hands grabbed them, pulled them apart, and down the mound toward the fire around the people.

"No! Oh, no!"

Everyone stopped and turned to the sound of Lord

Harleigh's voice. He was still on top of the mound. And even though the fire was behind him, suddenly a clear, bright light flashed across his face. He squinted. He held up his hands to shield his eyes from the glare. He staggered and almost fell.

Is it really true? Danny thought wildly. Does the doll really work? But then he turned with the others and saw where the light was coming from.

Two headlights were bouncing toward them across the plateau. They were moving very quickly, and soon the shape of the car was clear. Danny pushed his way through the stunned crowd to Lark. He grabbed Islington and pressed him against his chest. "It's Lil!" he said. "She's come to save us!"

THE TUMULI

23

The noise of the engine was the only sound. As the car drew closer the people huddled together. Suddenly they seemed embarrassed.

Lark and Danny stood close to each other, watching the car. Danny turned back briefly to look at Lord Harleigh. The lights had left him, and he was now only a scrawny shadow before the flames.

The car shuddered to a stop at the edge of the crowd. A tall bearded man stepped out. Lark ran into his arms. Two policemen leapt from the back, surveyed the scene, and hurried toward Lord Harleigh. Philippa emerged from the driver's seat, and Danny started toward her.

She gasped when she saw him. There were tears in her eyes. "Danny!" she cried. "Oh, my God, what happened to you?"

"The fire," he said, "Lord Harleigh threw Islington into the fire, and I pulled him out."

"*You* risked your life to save Islington? You? But, are you all right?"

"Yes, it's just my hair."

"And Islington?"

The cat's fur was blackened and curled, but he did not seem to be in pain. He rested comfortably against Danny's chest. Reluctantly, Danny handed him to Philippa, who cuddled him against her, rocking slowly back and forth. "My poor darling," she said softly to the cat, "at least I haven't lost you as well."

"As well . . . ?" Danny asked, but he knew what she meant, and a strange kind of joy, half mixed with sorrow, rose inside him.

The policemen were back now, each with a firm grip on Lord Harleigh's elbow. "Didn't even put up a struggle," one of them said. "Came as gentle as a baby, he did."

The other policeman spoke to Danny. "Young fellow, I wouldn't have been in your shoes for anything. And this poor girl!" Lark and her father had approached. His arm was around her, and she was wiping her face with the back of her hand. "No," the policeman went on, "I wouldn't have done what you did, and neither would anybody else around here. We've known about these goings-on for years. But nobody dared to interfere with this fellow." He shook Lord Harleigh's arm. "His family's been in control in these parts for centuries. Just look at all the followers he has, all these poor, misguided people whose lives he runs." Lord Harleigh snorted. "They live in fear of him, I can tell you."

Danny searched for the librarian, and thought he saw him crouching behind a shivering group of fat ladies. "But we could never take steps. We never had proof that he did anything against the law, and so many people were involved who he can get to do anything for him, anything." The policeman paused and cleared his throat. "But *tonight*, why, we *had* to come here, we had to stop this thing, once we heard you children were here, and possibly in danger. There was nothing else we could do. If it weren't for you, young man, and the girl, why this might have kept going on and on. But because of you, we had to put a stop to it."

"Sniveling adolescent," Lord Harleigh murmured, but no one seemed to hear him.

"I don't know what to say," Danny said. "I suppose it was dangerous. I just had to find out what was going on here."

"I must say," said Lark's father, "I wasn't particularly pleased when I heard you two were up here." His voice was deep and rather rough. "But I know my daughter. She's just as foolhardy as they come."

Lark looked up at him. "But what happened? How did you get here so soon?"

"Well, I *was* worried. You've always been curious about things, and I knew the two of you were up to something. I was almost sure you had come up here, and I was furious." He shook her gently. "But just when I was really getting frantic, I heard a knock on the door, and Philippa stumbled in. I knew who she was immediately." He looked at her. She still seemed rather dazed. "And the whole story came out. Philippa had a good wash with cold water, and I rang the police."

"We're always on the alert on one of these nights," the policeman said, "just in case, you know." He turned back to face the huddled, confused crowd. "We'd better get going. We'll have to take your car, ma'am, to get his lordship down to the station."

"Of course," Philippa mumbled.

He raised his voice to speak to the others. "All you people, go on home now. We're going to forget about most of you, pretend we never saw you here. Unless anything like this starts up again, then we'll know who to look for. And there's some of you, you know who you are, who better get out of this county, and quick, or you'll end up behind bars for a long, long time. Get on, now!" In groups, they began to move slowly away. "And one more thing, young man. What did they do with you here? How did your hair get burned? Did they try to hurt you?"

"Be careful, you little fool!" Lord Harleigh whispered hoarsely.

"Shut it!" snapped the policeman. "Ignore him. He can't do no witchcraft in jail."

"Well," Danny said, "yes, they did try. After Lord Harleigh threw the cat in the fire, and after I got him out—that's how I burned my hair—it all went so fast, it's a bit confused in my head—I burned this doll that was supposed to be magic. And Lord Harleigh sort of went crazy and made the people grab us, to throw *us* in the fire—and just then you got here."

"Oh, my God," Lark's father said, and tightened his arm around her.

"That's plenty to hold him on, plenty," said the policeman. "This fellow will be out of mischief for years to come. And not in a prison, I'll bet you. In hospital." Briskly, he snapped a pair of handcuffs on Lord Harleigh's wrists, and in a moment the car was hurrying back across the plateau. Almost all the people were gone, and the fires were dying away.

"Well, I guess we should start back," Danny said. He felt curiously light, as though at any moment he might simply float into the sky. "What time is it, anyway?"

"It must be almost morning," Lark's father said. And as Danny looked back one last time across the plateau he saw a pale glow beginning to creep over the tops of the hills.

They tramped in silence through the muddy places and out onto the track. Danny's mind was empty; all he could think about was the countryside around them, and as they walked he studied it more carefully than ever before. Everything was gray or black in the pre-dawn light, and the forest on the left was just beginning to separate into distinct trees. It was almost as though what had just happened was a dream, until Lark, walking beside him, said, "Hey, we did it, didn't we? It's all over now, we found out everything, and didn't it turn out perfect, though?"

"It almost didn't turn out at all," Lark's father said. "It's damn lucky we got there when we did, I can tell you." He sounded a bit irritated.

"But how *did* you get there, in Lil, I mean?" Danny asked.

Philippa, walking with her head bowed, and Islington pressed tightly against her, did not answer. So in a moment

Lark's father said, "The police picked us up outside the Black Swan, then drove up the hill. We had to go past Blackbriar, that's the only road up the hill, you know. Their car just barely made it to the house. They said it had already been up there once this evening . . ."

"Oh, yes," Danny said, remembering Mr. Bexford.

"And the thing just died right outside the front door. We were frantic, but Philippa's car started right up."

They had almost reached the end of the track, and the morning light was stronger. Lark's father looked closely at Danny and shook his head. "You know," he said, "I wouldn't have recognized you at all from Lark's description. She said you were skinny and pale, but you're just as robust and ruddy as a young farmhand."

"I guess I've changed," said Danny.

"You certainly have," Philippa said.

"Oh, it was the country," Lark said. "I know it."

"And I suppose all your daring exploits had something to do with it too," Philippa added.

"And Mary Peachy," said Danny. "I just have the feeling that part of her is still at Blackbriar, and somehow it got through to me."

"Oh, come off it," said Philippa. "You don't believe in ghosts."

But the events of the night had been so fantastic, so unreal, that what Danny was saying about Mary Peachy hardly seemed strange to him at all. "I don't really, but you yourself—" He stopped abruptly.

"What about me?"

Why shouldn't I tell her? Danny thought. "You were

afraid of her doll. You felt something from it. It had some kind of power over you. I didn't throw it away, and I was never afraid of it. It had a different power over me."

"That's what I told you," Lark said.

"I know. It's a lucky thing I didn't throw it away. No wonder you hated it, Philippa. I'm sure it was other things, too, but if it hadn't been for that doll, and Mary Peachy, I'd probably still be—"

But this time he knew he shouldn't finish. They stepped out of the pine thicket, and stopped.

The house itself looked no different than it had the first time they had seen it. Still a part of the earth, it seemed just as bleak and gray and desolate as ever. But as they stood there, the sun appeared over the edge of the hill and touched the house with a rich glow that made the flint walls look warm for the first time. And overnight, the yard around it had become a blanket of tiny blue flowers.

EPILOGUE

Danny went back to London with Mr. Bexford. It should have been an unpleasant train ride, but Danny stared out the window the whole time in a warm, happy daze. Once in London, he insisted on going to a school in the country, and Mr. Bexford finally agreed that the problem of finding him a place to live could most easily be solved by sending him to a boarding school. He chose one with green fields and crumbling medieval buildings, and though his life there was not quite as exciting as it had been at Blackbriar, it was stimulating enough, in many new ways, to keep him very busy for the next few years.

Philippa did not try to persuade him to stay with her. After a few lost, lonely days she woke up one morning with a brilliant idea. She gathered together all the money she had left, and bought a small shop in Dunchester. Doing much of the work herself, she made it over into a restaurant.

The food she spent hours preparing was so much more delicious than anything else available in Dunchester that the restaurant soon provided her with a comfortable income. She had a small staff who followed all her orders to the letter, and not once did any of them drop a single pie. Islington's coat soon grew back, and he was just as beautiful as he had always been. Lark's father, and even Lark herself, became her good friends, and often visited her in her little apartment above the restaurant.

On occasional weekends she would pick Danny up in Lil and bring him back to visit Blackbriar. They never stayed long, and soon stopped entering the house at all. Year by year tiles dropped off the roof, windowpanes cracked, and the forest crept slowly into the yard.

And for years to come, Danny could not forget the sound of Mary Peachy's voice. He often wondered if, on winter nights, it still echoed past the cold fireplaces, through the empty rooms of the house that would always belong to her alone.